THE MEN'S MEETING

A novella by Kathleen Box

Chapters

Matching Song List

1. Tighten Up – The Black Keys
2. Sound and Color – Alabama Shakes
3. Freshman – Verve
4. The Summer - Citizen
5. Sail – Awolnation
6. Royals – Lorde
7. I Am...I said – Neil Diamond
8. I'm Not the One – The Cars
9. The Space Between – Dave Matthews Band
10. Lies – Glen Hansard
11. Wonderful - Everclear
12. Come Undone – Duran Duran
13. Bring Me to Life - Evanescence
14. Hallelujah - Jeff Buckley
15. Secrets – One Republic
16. I Wanna Get Better – Bleachers
17. Try Again – Aaliyah
    Radioactive - Imagine Dragons
    Turn Down For What – DJ Snake
    We're Up All Night – Daft Punk
    Peaceful World – John Mellancamp

18. Copa Cabana – Manilow VS Gimme Shelter – The Rolling Stones
19. Steal My Sunshine - Len
20. Classic Man – Jidanna
21. I Wanna Get Better – Bleachers
22. Thinking Out Loud – Ed Sheeran
    Mr. Brightside - Killers
23. None
24. Sailing – Christopher Cross
25. Let Her Go – Passenger
26. Freshman – Verve
27. Take Me to Church – Hoozier
28. Hallelujah - Panic at the Disco
29. Killer Queen - Queen
30. Solar Eclipse – Seahaven
31. Solar Eclipse – Seahaven (continued)
32. Wouldn't It Be Lovely – My Fair Lady

Matt, after serving ten years in the military, found himself looking for work. The placement secretary at the local Veterans Administration job fair suggested he try his hand at a recent opening as a home inspector.

Matt was quite suited for it. The guys, his new coworkers are welcoming but his cross manner of speech makes them uncomfortable in front of the potential homeowners.

The company was inspecting a 1960's high ranch for a couple in their late twenties. Nervous and excited about purchasing their first home, Matt asked them if they planned on having children?

"Yes." They smiled at each other that they had answered in unison.

"That's sweet." Matt flashed his naturally soothing grin, and probably should have stopped there. Instead, he continued, "Well in an old house like this with a gas line over the years erosion may have occurred in the copper lines. You're going to want to hard wire in a carbon monoxide alert system connected to an alarm contract in case of a gas leak. Though the gas itself leaves an odor, the carbon monoxide can fill a house swiftly with little warning. Do you sleep with the windows open?"

"No." They again responded in unison with flat expressions.

"Of course not. People have the air conditioning on in the summer and the heat in the winter leaving the house as a little container for carbon monoxide build up. It only takes a few hours and the symptoms are barely noticeable. Headache maybe, pop a couple of Motrin and off to bed."

They stare at him with concern.

"There'd be nothing worse than child rearing those little cherubs only to find one day none of you wake up. Just are found blue and lifeless, stiff and peaceful in your beds because you save a few bucks thinking it could never happen to us."

Then he laughs, "Just kidding. Not really though, you should invest in smoke and carbon monoxide detectors."

He continued this way, on this and every home inspection. He was right to inform them, he argued with the coworkers. The company just wanted him to lighten up a little. People don't want to hear 'worst case scenarios' when they are buying their 'dream home'. Matt didn't understand, he thought this was his job, inspect and inform the customer. He did his best to hold his tongue and took to just writing down the issues and letting his partner do the talking. It was working out better now.

The summer heat arrived early, though it was spring.

Matt lived in a boarding house just off a main street in Hempstead. He could afford a better place in a better neighborhood but something about the activity and noise he found comforting. He'd never been alone, his whole life he'd been surrounded by people and a quiet home would mean boredom and boredom for him was just short of death.

All the boarders had issues. That was the nature of being a boarder. They all shared the kitchen, living room, and two bathrooms. Each had their own locked bedroom so if you wanted to be alone or didn't want to watch whatever mindless T.V. show they had chosen, you could lock yourself away.

A young couple in their early twenties occupied the room next to his in the boarding house. The guy must have been a drug dealer because for the amount of time he spent stumbling and sleeping around the house. He owned a beautiful brand new sports car, a black Ford Mustang with a spoiler and sweet rims. They were into taking drugs themselves, drinking, and sleeping at all hours of the day and through the night. The boyfriend was aggressive, and the more he drank the more belligerent he became. He was usually just verbally abusive and that the girlfriend seemed to handle with shouting back or crying until he apologized or stormed out. Matt often lay on his neatly made bed and listened to their drama through plaster walls.

One night though, the argument was heated and they must have done some heavy drugs, meth perhaps, their words were slurred but vicious. Matt tried to find relief from the heat and humidity, soothe the sweaty sheets and drown out their shouts with his oscillating fan on full blast. When the shattering of glass, her screams grew high pitched and the yelling and thumps against his wall became intolerable, he grabbed his pistol and loaded. He banged on their door, but walked away headed down the stairs and out the front door.

"What you want?' The boyfriend yelled to Matt's back and followed him out. "This is between me and my bitch. Mind your own fucking business. Where you going pussy? You got something to say? Say it. I'll fuck you up."

Matt turned on the small front lawn. The pistol gleamed at his side under the streetlight.

"You gonna shoot me. What the fuck is wrong with you soldier boy?" The boyfriend backed up with his hands in the air. "Alright, man. Be cool. I'm chill. I'm chill."

Matt turned and shot out the windows and tires of the Mustang. The boyfriend acted as if he had been shot. He begged Matt to stop.

"No." Matt said flatly. "Get the fuck out."

"Where am I going to go? You shot my car man. You're crazy." Matt held the gun to his head.

"I'm what?"

He didn't answer.

The police were called. Sympathetic to Matt, being a veteran, they explained the process. They searched his room, he had a collection of two rifles and a shotgun but that was his only pistol and he had a carry permit for it. They had to arrest him for the shooting of a car but the other guns were registered and would not be an issue. He'd spend the night in jail and have a hearing in the morning. Matt agreed cooperatively, they didn't even handcuff him as he got in the vehicle willingly. They chatted on the ride and thanked him for his service to our country. A night in jail was no different than a night in a houseful of kids, barracks, or boarding house. He'd sleep fine.

The house was searched. The dealer's room had an extensive amount of pot, heroin, meth, and illegal weapons. Him and the girlfriend were taken away in handcuffs. The drugs found in the trunk and door panels of the Mustang led it to be impounded as evidence.

Matt made his court appearance at Nassau County courthouse in Mineola, New York. He had one ear bud in listening to *'Freshman' by the Verve*. The other ear exposed, waiting for his name to be called.

Matt waited on a bench in the dimly lit hallway of the courthouse.

"Matthew Hall?" Arnold Feinman Esquire called out to his next client. Arnold is doing a group of pro bono cases today. Matt's tall lean muscular physique towers over Arnold's small stature. Matt greets him with a firm handshake that Arnold felt could easily crush a man. They enter the courtroom and sit together at the defendant's table. He quickly reviews Matt's file before the hearing.

Scanning the highlighted notes of the case documents, Arnold questions Matt. "You gave a snack bar to another serviceman when you knew he had a nut allergy?"

"Yes." Matt giggles. "Oh, you should've seen his face. Blew up like a cartoon character. I saved him though. He had an epi-pen He was fine. He came back two days later, like a free vacation. He's still an asshole though."

"You put hair remover in the shampoo dispenser?"

Matt "I never understood why someone sent us that. They packed a whole case of it really. There weren't even women at our base camp. Not even a gay."

Arnold looks up to face Matt directly, "You mean not even a gay person."

"Yeah, that's what I said, a gay."

They exchange annoyed glances, each thinking the other is an idiot.

Arnold continues, "You shot a car?'

"Yes sir." Matt nodded enthusiastically. "A 2014 black Ford Mustang with a spoiler, sweet rims and…"

Arnold interrupts, "With the prevalence of PTSD and over diagnosis of scripts, blaming your behavior on the psychotropic drugs …wait, what did they have you on?" he questions as he flips the pages of Matt's file.

"Nothing." Matt shrugged.

"The last thing they want is convictions against our 'homecoming heroes'." He makes quotation marks gesture. "Look, what you've done is a little criminal." Arnold's palms face up as he shrugs.

"Trying to kill my comrades is a little criminal?" Matt tilts his head inquisitively.

"I didn't hear that." Arnold gestures blocking his ear. " The hospitals are already overcrowded. I can get you out of this without a scratch."

Matt "I want the hospital."

Arnold Feinman leans in and lectures Matt, "No you don't. It's a mess, back logs, incompetent doctors, Obama's fucked this system… they throw some pills at you and you're another zombie, a forgotten veteran, you sit in a confined bland room and fight for the remote to watch television. Not even the good channels. They serve you shit hospital food and make you walk circles in a courtyard. That's not a life. It's fucked up." He taps the pen in his hand on the desk to emphasize his main points.

"Watch your mouth." Matt said with a straight face.

"You're kidding me right?'

Matt grins, "Yeah, I don't give a fuck."

Arnold sighed, "Geez. Honestly half these guys would be better off in prison."

Matt nods in agreement, " Okay, get me that. Prison."

"These are minor offenses and you almost killed a guy…but shooting a car of a known convicted drug dealer. Not really offensive?"

"Three guys." Matt states confidently.

"I didn't hear that." Gestures blocked ear again.

Matt repeats slightly louder, "Three guys."

Arnold Feinman eyes the pile of files before him, a heavy caseload today. "Don't sweat it. You'll be out of here by lunch."

"Sir?"

"You don't have to call me sir."

"And then what?" Matt genuinely doesn't know.

"Go home. Meet your girlfriend. You've got a girlfriend?"

Matt shakes his head dismissively.

Arnold continues speaking over him, " Go to work, work out, sit on the couch, play video games. You're one of the lucky ones. You wouldn't believe the mess…" Arnold pauses, his head resting on his chin, "The conditions these guys are coming back in. They're just shells of men. You. You. You're one of the 'lucky ones'. "

'Lucky ones', Matt reflects.

Matt heard the cries of his comrades and the echo of a firefight. He felt the cold sand whip across his skin. He watched, in his minds eye, him and his best friend, Cameron, are walking in the cold desert winds of Afghanistan and a herd of goats pass, women in black burkas move aside not making eye contact. The guys joke about smelling fish in the air when there isn't a fishing hole for miles. Was it the dung coals burning?

Patrolling the area, they step onto the crackling dirt of the road exiting the small village. The explosion threw Matt to the ground. It left a deafening ringing in his head. As the dust cleared, he lifted his head slowly and saw Cameron's hand. Relieved he reached out to grab it.

"Cam, you alright?" It was just a hand. Matt held it close and drew himself up to search around for the rest of him. The roadside bomb had scattered Cameron's parts. Matt scanned for pieces and gathered them up, a torso, a helmet with part of his face eyes open mouth agape, a boot with his leg up to the knee attached. He gathered them all. It was getting heavy. Other marines were running towards them. They slowed, mouthing words he couldn't hear. The ringing. He carried his "brother" towards them with his arm outstretched showing them the hand. The gray faded to black.

Matt woke in a bright make shift hospital room. "Shrapnel was removed.
You'll be back to work tomorrow. You're one of the lucky ones." The doctor's
voice was firm, encouraging, over the still ringing in his ears

Arnold continued, "Says you had four injuries in two tours and you returned to combat within days. God is really looking out for you. If you believe that sort of thing."

"I do sir. I've known Jesus as my Lord and Savior since my mother first introduced us to the word of God."

"Well, I'm more of an Old Testament guy, myself. But I respect all faiths. Except Muslims, but you didn't hear that from me."

"Yes, I did. Are you one of them Jews? I've never met a real Jew before."

Arnold's mouth drops open, "Seriously? Well you're in New York now, kid, you're going to meet a lot of us. Just so you know, we prefer to be called Jewish, and we migrate to Florida in the winter."

Matt made a mental note, "Okay."

"I'm joking…kind of." Arnold flips his hand. Matt notices he talks with his hands, a lot, like a puppet.

"Okay, I want to go to prison." Matt said calmly.

"No you don't. A pretty boy like you will be somebody's bitch within an hour. I'll work this out. You like video games?" Arnold's hands wave over the file dismissively.

"Pardon sir? I'll take the hospital."

"There's a waiting list and this all works in your favor anyway. Take advantage, you have an out. You're not suicidal are you?"

Matt shakes head fervently "No."

"Let me do my job and get you out of here." Arnold is firm.

"What if I told you I killed someone?"

Arnold shrugs dismissively, "Of course you did. You're a soldier."

The Judge enters. The room quiets. "All rise."

The verdict is guilty Matt's pistol permit is temporarily revoked until the completion of required "anger management" course.

In the hallway of the courthouse at lunchtime the stir of voices bounce off the marble walls. The steps of people moving about sound tinny and echo. Matt is furious with Arnold Feinman. Matt wanted to be admitted to a psych ward. The attorney sarcastically suggests that he would have to 'practically kill somebody'. This calms Matt down.

Arnold Feinman turns away and calls out the name of his next defendant.

When he arrives home, Matt appreciates the quiet. They wouldn't be back.

He pulls out a computer manual and begins the process of downloading a variety of updated applications. The room is strewn with computer parts and wiring all carefully sorted and labeled.

The splashing water echoed off the marble walls. Matt leaned his free hand on the cold porcelain. Father Giovanni glanced down at Matt. Matt looked out of the corner of his eye avoiding direct contact. Matt acknowledged his presence with a nod. He shook the dampness that spilled on his work boots.

The tall leather bound door swung open and startled both of them. A small-framed woman in a plaid suit looked startled to see them in the quiet as well.

"Oh, hello Father." She clutched tissues in one hand with her bag hanging in the crook of her arm. She made a downward glance at the abundance of water flowing.

She studied the young man and the collection of milk jugs Matt was filling with holy water from the large font at the back of the church.

She said in a prim voice, "Young man, are you going to take all the water?"

Father Giovanni gently waved his hand in a manner to hush her. Matt's steel blue eyes caught hers and he feigned a painful smile. She scurried out the back doors.

Matt noticed Father Giovanni quickly sizing up his obvious faded military T-shirt, worn by numerous returning veterans, a staple in their wardrobe, and Matt's World Trade Center tattoo peeked out from under the half sleeve.

Father Giovanni softly approached Matt. "Are you alright son?"

Matt smiled.

"If you ever need to talk, I am here for you."

"Thank you Father." Matt responded flatly. Couldn't the priest see he was very busy right now?

Matt lifted the last of the seven gallons of containers to the spigot and continued filling. The font was spilling out slowly now. The water was running low. Matt wasn't one for small talk and he was growing uncomfortable with Father Giovanni's presence.

His shoulders flinched and he stretched and rolled his shoulders, tilting his head back while studying the ornate gold gilt painted ceiling.

Father Giovanni took the hint and continued about the business of church work. His daily routine soon coming to an end, it was time to shut off the electric candles people paid a dollar to light in prayer.

Matt capped and took the jugs out to his white work van, two by two. He parked directly in front of the church blocking the crosswalk. He propped the wide back doors open and made multiple trips as he organized the collection, holding it in place with his loaded duffle bag, so as not to let them spill over. The magnetic company logo hung a little slanted on the back door. He peeled and the readjusted it.

Peter works as a plumber at a sewage treatment plant. He is always sloppily dressed in his work attire. Though he is unshaven with wild shoulder length dirty blond hair, he is always smiling and joking with fellow workers. They like him.

Heading out to his car during their lunch break, Peter picks up a key from the ground and studies it. He makes good money, but drives a crappy old station wagon. He opens the rear hatch to put the key in a bucket he has already filled with discarded keys. The car is filled with tools, gadgets, facemasks, rubber gloves, and various items he finds. The front passenger seat covered with fast food bags, water bottles, Snapple, papers, notes, and magazines made it impossible for anyone to join him.

He drives to meet guys from work at local pub they go to because they smell bad from work. They look in his car before heading in. One of the guys, sarcastically comments on the garbage in his car, says, "That's how you get all the ladies, huh, Peter? Impressing them with your swerve ride?" The others laugh as they eyeball the beat up vehicle and its hoard.

"Why don't you throw it out, it's just garbage?" another friend chimed in. "The whole car should be driven and scrapped at the dump. I bet you'd get a couple bucks. By a couple I mean two." They all laugh.

Peter smiles.

Anxiety takes a hold of him as the memories rush back. 'Garbage', he is garbage. When he was a young boy, about eight years old, his adoptive parents are telling him 'the story' of how he was found.

The sounds of a crying baby were heard above the commotion of the New York City subway station. Someone searched the metal garbage pail risking the exposure to germs. He was just a few hours old and premature. They saw this little bloody mess of a child wrapped in a green plastic garbage bag. An ambulance and the newspapers were called. They showed him the news clippings of a Police Officer cradling him in the midst of a crowd waiting for the next train. A miracle, really, his mother claimed tearfully.

His adoptive mother worked as a nurse in the hospital he was brought to. She cared for him through the whole process of his recovery and fell in love, she told him so sympathetically. They adopted him and brought him home to this family. He was so lucky, so blessed.

Presently, he looks around at garbage pails and the contents of the car. He can hear the woosh of blood in his ears, he gets dizzy and his anxiety rises. The pounding in his chest is all too familiar. Peter grabs cell phone to call his therapist Jason. It goes to voicemail, "I need help."

When Peter was dining on pub food, he always ordered an extra meal 'to go'. He brought the bag outside where he'd sit with Jack, a homeless man he'd befriended over the last few years. Jack was often a little buzzed from the drink, and his lazy eye always wandered as he spoke. His dirty clothes, wrinkled and worn, meant little to Peter when Jack greeted him with a warm smile.

"That could've been me, lost to the world." Peter always thought to himself.

The greeting was always the same. "How you doing Jack?"

"Jack be nimble, Jack be quick, Jack be a simple man, but Jack's not a dick!" He'd laugh at his own joke as if he told it for the first time. Every time.

Peter handed him the bag of fried food and a sandwich. Then took a spot on a flattened cardboard box next to Jack on the sidewalk, leaning his back against the wooden shingles under the neon lit windows of the bar.

Peter sipped his coke as Jack ate sloppily beside him. It was a Monday and this may be the only meal Jack had since Friday. They talked about the weather. For Peter it was just a change of clothing and turning from AC to heating. For Jack, it was a change in survival mode. His tent in the woods by the pond would not sustain him soon. He'd looked into a shelter but it was far away. Two bus rides, he explained, and it was in a bad neighborhood. He liked it here. Nobody mugged him, and there are pretty views. He often walked the park trails, pushing a cart of belongings, and dragging his limp leg behind him. Peter never asked about the limp anymore.

Jack withdrew when it came up and would only quietly respond, "Shit happens kid."

Jack was going to find somewhere local to spend his winter this year. He was accumulating a sleeping bag, boxes, blankets, matches and tarps. The cart was piled high and left in a narrow alleyway. There wasn't an abundance of homeless people in the area. Jack was their guy and this was a gesture, not really looking out for him, but not abandoning him either.

"When you going to get a nice girl and settle down Peter?"

"What makes you think I don't?"

"A woman changes a man Peter. Makes you smile a little more. Motivational, they are."

Peter was lonely. He went to night school for training required by his job. He met a nice girl that was taking a class across the hall from his class. They chatted in the hall a few times, he walked her to her car and they'd exchanged numbers. Their conversations were light and happy. He asked her to dinner and she seemed annoyed with his car. He knew enough to move things out of the passenger seat. She complained it smelled funny and was sticky. He said he should have listened to his mother and borrowed his parents' car. He caught himself and said they weren't really his parents. As the night went on he ended up telling her his history.

He wept a little, she seemed so understanding and positive about it, "God meant you to be a gift for someone else, that's all." Her big brown eyes shined with enthusiasm.

The next time he saw her she was kind but didn't want him to walk her out. She was "Fine, thanks."

His mother suggested he send flowers but he didn't have an address. He thought of her every day and night that week.

He sent a vase of flowers delivered to her classroom. He watched from the hall. She was flustered in the middle of an exam. When she opened the card, it simply read "I Love You, Peter".

Her hands were shaking and she accidently knocked the vase over, it shattered. She apologized to the class as she cleaned up the mess and colorful array of flowers strewn about the floor. The teacher was annoyed and did not allot extra test time. Peter hid from her view. At the end of class, he approached her on the stairwell.

"I'm sorry Peter, I'm seeing someone else." She said sweetly.

He didn't understand women at all.

"I don't understand women, Jack." Peter said flatly.

"No one does, Peter. But you will, when it's the right one. It's easy. Magical really."

"Were you ever married Jack?"

"Once. His brown eyes with the yellowing signs of jaundice seemed to straighten as he focused on a sign across the street. Peter knew that's not what Jack saw in his minds eye though. "Lost her to the cancer, seven years ago."
After a long pause Peter said, "I'm sorry Jack."

Jack chuckled, "So here I am. Cancer took my wife, bills took my home, grief took my job." Jack continued eating as he spoke. "But a woman, Peter, that's a beautiful thing. She's not here but she's here." And he patted his sandwich to his heart with his dirty hands.

Johnny works as an auto body mechanic for a local gas station in an industrial park just outside of town. To make the day go faster the radio is always on. Today *Lorde 'Royals'* plays in the background. Johnny's boss is breaking his balls, Johnny laughs even though he's not listening, but inside Johnny is disgusted. His father was a ball breaker and he hates that type of sadistic personality, but work is work, so he tolerates it. He has a family to support. Johnny, usually good natured, is agitated now. He's working so hard to support his family. Seems like they can never get ahead. He regrets his years of drinking and smoking pot. So much money and time wasted in dark rooms and little memory of them. He adores his wife Annie and can't stand the disappointment in her eyes when he has to so often say, "We can't afford it."

Annie is kind with her tone and responses, but he can't help this gut feeling of failure. She deserves better than that, if he knows that then she does too. He's afraid one day she'll find a man that's a better provider and walk out that door. Images of her on exotic vacations and fancy cars and her and this 'mystery man' play out like a commercial in his mind. She's not like that, those things aren't important to her. She said so, many times. He believed her when she spoke those words, but when he was alone his insecurities, they played with his mind.

He looks at the calendar, no one knows but he is marking the calendar for number of days of sobriety. It'll be three years this weekend. He pulls the AA coin from his pocket runs it though fingers and puts it away. He steps outside to smoke. He daydreams of his wife and kids getting ready that morning. Just an ordinary day, very routine, he likes that, it's soothing.

The daydream is broken when a pretty young woman approaches him. She is slightly agitated and slightly flirtatious. Johnny is a handsome man and women feel at ease with his strong yet mild mannerisms. Johnny doesn't know how to take her. They go inside the shop and he summarizes the bill and tells her the amount for the repair.

She angers swiftly, beginning a verbal assault, "Nobody called and told me that. You assholes can't just bill me without calling. I never approved...", she continues, her voice rising with each sentence, "My insurance won't cover...".

Johnny watches her lips move but the harsh words block the beauty of her face. He is overly defensive and tells her to "Shut the fuck up."

His boss hears the commotion from behind the glass door to the garage. He quickly intervenes, telling Johnny to calm down and go back to the repairs.

Johnny starts to work, but can't concentrate, embarrassed by his outburst. It angers him and he starts to throw shit around. First a wrench is tossed, then a tire grabbed and flung into the open area of the lot. He rips a metal sign off the wall cutting his finger in the process and starts to kick, bend and destroy it.

"What the hell are you doing Johnny?" a voice booms. It's his boss.

Johnny pauses and looks around for a moment. The bitch is standing behind the boss in the doorway with her mouth agape.

"Sorry." He hangs his head. "I'm going to need a break."

"Whatever." The boss shakes his head in disbelief. "Clean it up when you get back."

"Yeah. Okay." Johnny heads to a public parking lot next door and lights another cigarette. He wipes his bloody finger on his work pants.

After a moment, he pauses, takes out cell phone. He calls Jason, "I need help."

Bill is up early, going to work a shift as a steamfitter. He earns substantial wages but hides it in a bank account, statements sent to his mother's address. He is selfish. He is married to a 9-11 widow of a firefighter. Statues and tributes are about the house. He is awoken to the sound of his wife Rebecca agitated with the garbage disposal not working. He opens his eyes with dread. Bill heavily lumbers downstairs to the kitchen of the typical yet oversized suburban home.

"I'll fix it when I have time."

"You always say that there's never time." She snapped.

Argument ensues that she's going to have to hire someone, yet again. He promises it will get done.

That day, Bill takes a break from his welding job at Laguardia Airport.

"Where did I leave my phone?" he asks his partner. Panic rushes over him. Today she would find it. His secrets would be out. The secrets he'd been so careful to keep close to himself.

She was too fat, too stupid, too lazy, too in love, to see he had all along been with other women, sometimes just a girlfriend on the side and sometimes orgies. He does the right thing, though, wearing a condom with the others, because he's a good guy, she doesn't appreciate that.

Thank goodness he locked a pass code on his phone, she'd never guess it's his mother's birthday. His mother never liked Rebecca and thought he was too good for her. She understood and let him meet his lovers in her basement. It was none of Rebecca's business anyway. His current girlfriend called on his cell phone. He scrambled to find the buzzing phone in his overall pocket. She tells him how sweet he is and she misses him, his heart melts at her sweetness.

That evening, he lay on the couch in the cool darkness of the room. The T.V. was on to distract him from his thoughts but he muted it when it only made the chatter of his own mind louder and repetitive.

Work in the heat had beaten him down today and it was difficult to bend the fat fingers of his work worn hands. Her homes air conditioning brought little relief from the heat of his body. Beads of sweat still ran down his face even after a cool dip in her pool.

There was much to be tackled on the 'to do' list today, Rebecca will take care of it, she always does. Bill had only one desire. He thought of her, his girlfriend, and her youthful innocent ways. How her lashes flitted when she laughed and her tongue was so soft on his lips. These words she sends, teasing him, arousing him. The only 'to do' was to satisfy his desire for her. He covered himself with a blanket even though the heat was too much. Just as her scantily clad photo popped up on his phone screen he heard the key in the door. Rage and embarrassment consumed him, his temperature rose.

Rebecca kicked off and tossed her sandals on the mat by the front door. They now joined the pile of different styles and sizes of the family feet. There were more shoes than people.

The gray and blue glow of the distant unlit living room let her know that he was home and settled in on the couch again.

She heard the click clicking of his phone keypad over the muted television.

She had picked up necessities and some of Bill's favorites to make him feel special. She gently put the groceries away and now empty bags into a bag holder under the sink. Order, that's all we need, once everything is in order it will all be okay.

She stepped barefoot across the stone floor, and was surprised by the darkness she was entering on such a sunny day. All the curtains were drawn.

Bill heard his wife banging around the kitchen. The crumpling of plastic bags annoyed him. He heard her stomp across the floor to the foot of the couch. He jumped acting startled as if he were just now disrupted from a deep sleep.

She wouldn't ask him for help today. He worked hard. It can wait.

"How are you?" She sat at his side to kiss his head. "You're burning up."

"I know! I work!" He snapped.

She pulled back and saw his phone lay flat face down, on his bloated belly.

As she stood to leave the room, he touched her hand. They clasped for a moment.

"What's for dinner?" Bill asked flatly.

The phone chimed, he didn't look at it. Rebecca knew what that meant. She wasn't as stupid as he thought. Their hands released. She stepped away softly, silently.

He sat up angry at the way she stormed out.

Then, he checked his phone. What a sweet girl.

CHAPTER 8 – THOMAS

Thomas lies in his apartment with large windows. He takes for granted the amazing views over Central Park and of the city's night skyline, from his posh suite at The Majestic 115 Central Park West in Lincoln Square, New York City. Everything is neat, gray hues, and suits line the opulent closet. He came from old money and had an affinity for the finer things in life. Prescription drugs were easy to come by, just a call to 'the family doctor', no questions asked.

His ex-wife had accused him of domestic violence. He denied it, of course, but the truth was he didn't remember. He was highly functional, performed his job as a high end Manhattan realtor with excellence. He had the plaques and trophies displayed in his office to show for it. After hours, though, sometimes life was a blur.

She left him after a heated argument. That he knew. How the porcelain vases, Waterford crystal had landed on the marble floors and a collection of fine art in the fireplace? He did not recall. He was remanded in divorce court to attend 'anger management' and was served an order of protection.

Tonight, Thomas is having sex with current girlfriend. She's high end, and high maintenance, but he enjoys her company. He fades in and out of picturing his ex-wife. Thomas shouts out her name. His girlfriend leapt out of bed and they fight as she gathered all her clothes from the floor.

She said, "You don't know what it's like to love somebody that doesn't love you!" Tearful and angry she sits on the edge of the bed, dressing in long silence, "You want her, go get her." She slams the door behind her as she leaves.

Thomas goes into bathroom shouting out loud. "This fucking bitch. What the fuck! I don't need this shit!" He smashes the mirror in the bathroom and then knocks all the items off the granite countertop and onto the kitchen floor. He takes two diazapam and a shot of fine bourbon to wash it down. Thomas sleeps well.

The next morning, Thomas sees the mess, blood on the sheets and broken glass. Calls therapist. "I need help".

CHAPTER 9 - DAMIEN

Damien, in his forties, is a conceited yet insecure New York City firefighter, a man of many obsessions: the attention of women, food, work, technology, working out and hobbies. His appetite for attention is insatiable. He breaks off relationships as soon as someone gets close to seeing his flaws. The obsession with technology distracts him constantly, even at work he texts multiple women at the same time and gets notifications from Facebook, the local firehouse he volunteers at in his home town, Twitter, Instagram, etc. Damien comes off cocky, but knows he's a loser, always wanting what he can't have.

Divorced for years now, he lives with his father, because he is terrible at managing money. They argue often about this since his mother passed away and the father always loses the battle. Damien feels entitled to live there for free because he's his son and his parents owe him from the abuse they dished out all those years. "It's your fault that I failed, nothing was ever good enough for you!" was the usually end to every confrontation. The father exhausted, defeated, let him stay and do 'chores' around the house as compensation.

Damien's at work, it's a slow day. His food obsession grips him and annoyingly he criticizes and takes over making lunch for the guys. They are helping. His comments come off cocky but the guys just call him a dick.

He is checking and texting multiple women.

He replays in his head, how he screwed everything up in his life. It can't be 'all my fault'. He soothes himself with a spoonful of food. He lost his ex-wife by cheating on her, he was honest about it and told her right away. She left him anyway, raked him over the coals in the process. It was an ugly divorce. She had him arrested on false pretenses. He had to take testosterone injections because years of steroid abuse had left his counts diminished. They had a daughter together and she won custody with the unfortunate bonus of a huge chunk of his income going to child support. He hates his ex-wife and yet tries to win her back, just to see if he can. Damien wouldn't commit again, he swore. So many years had passed but the title 'cheater' felt engraved on his heart.

"Once a cheater always a cheater." she had chanted. He believed her.

Over dinner, an argument breaks out about his constant distracted behavior at work. A firefighter calls him 'a loser' but the way the food is on his face around his mouth he envisions his mother's face, how she would eat and criticize him. The blood rushes, his heart beats heavy in his chest, he is on the defense. Damien is on testosterone injections, he's feeling pumped, he threatens to get physical with the guy. All the guys break them up saying 'what the fuck is wrong with you? Calm down.'

Damien retreats and leaves the kitchen. Text's Jason, "I need help."

Jason is a psychotherapist who has custody of his teenage daughter from his second divorce. He is currently in the process of his third. He finds it cathartic, divorce. He is gay. He won't admit it, not even to himself. Just because he sexually fantasizes about all his male patients and sleeps with men here and there, that doesn't make him gay, right?

His daughter had witnessed Jason's lover's slip out quietly in last night's clothes many times. 'Giggles' and 'call me' whispered on the front stoop while cheeky kisses were exchanged.

Jason and his daughter argue about her being allowed to spend the weekend at her friend's house.

"Yes there will be drinking." She snaps but answers honestly. "No the parents won't be home."

"Absolutely not! I forbid it!" he is sticking to his guns. It is the third day into this argument. His patience is wearing thin.

"Aren't you supposed to be the cool liberal Dad?" she mocks him. "You say I should be open about what I do with my friend's and my sexuality. Isn't that what you always say?"

"Yes. That doesn't mean I have to approve or condone your behavior—"

"But now you're behaving like an uptight librarian. That's what I get for being honest with you?"

He is getting ready for his 'Men's Meeting'. "I just can't do this right now." He looks at the time he has twenty minutes to review notes on the new member.

"Because," he explained in his calm mild mannered tone, "I repeatedly told you, an unsupervised party at your age is out of the question."

"I hate you! I wish I could live with my mother

"Your mother is in rehab. You want to live there?"

"It's your fault she's there!"

"How is it my fault?"

"Seriously Dad? You're gay! You've always been gay! You made her think she was 'craazzy' to the point where she was popping pills to just block you out!"

"You're just like your mother throwing that in my face!" he feels defeated. He takes a deep breath and continues, "I know you're angry, but that is a totally inappropriate accusation. You're mother has issues far beyond my control—" he says in his most controlled and condescending tone.

"Issues!" she yells. "She doesn't have issues, she had a passive-aggressive bitch for a husband!"

"We just weren't compatible. You know that.", he says sternly.

""Why? Because she doesn't have a cock that's why!"

In frustration he screams, "You're just like your mother! Out of control!"

She storms away. Slamming her bedroom door. She continues yelling "Gay! Gay! Gay!", from behind the closed door, while throwing things about her room.

Ten minutes, until the 'Men's Meeting'.

He looks at the words on the plaques on the wall. They are supposed to be 'healing' words of wisdom, now he is just annoyed by them.

Distracted from the argument, Jason couldn't concentrate on Matt's file. He put the folder in the file cabinet in his office. I'll get to it later, he thought to himself, probably just another PTSD case.

Matt arrived early. He was always early by nature and years of training. He is always prepared. He entered the downstairs back door of the wide high ranch home. The upstairs was Jason's private living quarters. The downstairs had a kitchen, half bath, small office that was locked, he checked, a small room for private sessions, and a larger room with a circle of fabric folding chairs. Matt was alone and studied the surroundings.

He stood waiting in the kitchen. The Keurig coffee maker was running. A wooden set of table and chairs to sit at is covered with a variety of 'self help' and 'spiritually motivational' books for patients to peruse while they wait.

Matt listens closely to the escalating argument between Jason and his daughter.

Thomas confidently walks in removing his light tan summer jacket neatly hanging it on the coat rack in the corner. He's dressed like a Brooks Brothers model and Matt is concerned he has underdressed for the meeting in his jeans and work boots. Thomas introduces himself as "Thomas, realtor extraordinaire!" with a toothy smile. He informs Matt that if he's ever looking for a place, "I'm your guy."

Matt notices the softness of Thomas' neatly manicured hand. A light but expensive cologne scent surrounds Thomas. Matt is unsure if he is in the right meeting.

"Is this a gay meeting?" he asks Thomas.

"What? No, Matt." Thomas tilts his head curiously.

Before Matt can ask more questions, the other members arrive through the back door, chatting heartily in deep masculine voices.

Introductions are made. Coffee is made. They chat lightly until Jason makes his soft smooth entrance and welcomes them to enter the large room, his palm gestured like the master of ceremony at a circus.

Matt hangs his well-worn denim jacket over the back of his seat. They all comfortably sit and wait for the one empty chair to be filled.

Johnny is late and rushes to sit, apology made.

"It's okay." Jason says softly.

Jason's voice is calm and controlled, as the group gathers for the Wednesday night "Men's Meeting". That's how it all began, patients that Jason saw individually that had similar emotional issues he invited to meet as a group. They all lack the ability to connect or express their emotional issues in a 'healthy' way. Jason felt as a group they could support one another. They hadn't really made any breakthroughs but Jason felt they all enjoyed the company and they had a safe place to speak.

Jason is secretly attracted to all of them and fantasizes regularly that an orgy will break out. He often offers to play the comforting 'mother' role. He gently praises them saying this is how a 'mother' or any 'woman' should treat a man.

Without any signs of flamboyance, Jason leads the group. Jason begins, by introducing Matt.

"Everyone we have a new member joining us this evening. Matthew." He gestures the intro with his palm up towards Matt sitting directly across the circle of chairs.

"It's Matt, Jay."

"Oh, I apologize, I just read your name directly from the file."

The group member introductions are made. When Jason says, "Lastly, I'm Jason."

Matt says, "Yes sir."

"You don't have to call me sir."

"Okay, Jay."

"Jason." he corrects him.

"Yes, sir, Jay."

Jason, though annoyed, ignores the purposeful error. Jason picks up on where they left off the previous week with Damien talking about the despair he feels living with his father, "Mr. Thorn", he refers to his father in quotation mark gesture, since the divorce.

Matt raises his eyebrows. "Wait, wait, wait a minute…"

All eyes turn to Matt.

"Your parents named you Damien Thorn?"

"Yes." Damien's face flushed.

"Damien Thorn from the 'Omen'?"

"Yes."

Matt laughs loudly, "No wonder you're all fucked up. Jesus. Who does that?"

Jason reprimands Matt, " I'm aware you are new to the group but it's out of line Matthew to interrupt and/or pass judgment on the other members. We treat each other with respect."

Matt, "Okay, but come on, isn't that an obvious problem? Did you ever think of changing your name?"

They are all serious and quiet. They've all thought it, but Matt was the first to state the obvious aloud.

Jason hold's his hand up slightly to hush Matt. "Feel free to continue Damien."

Damien continues complaining that his father wants him to pay his own way. Damien refuses because of legal fees and child support expenses. The father watches him rack up credit cards taking out dates and buying electronics. Damien complains both about missing his mother and hating her as well because he was never in her eyes, "enough".

Jason subtly asks, "How do you feel? Where do you feel it in your body?" The sweet soothing tone of Jason's voice brings Damien to tears. Bill cries too, he relates that he, too, feels he is never enough.

Matt observes.

Jason says in a meditative voice, "Let it out." He blows out a deep breath forcefully. "Let it go. Let it leave your body." They all follow, exhaling in unison with their eyes closed.

Matt still observes.

"Let the anger go, the resentment go." Jason opens his eyes to watch the men relax. Matt is staring blankly at him.

"Feel free to join us Matt. It's an exercise in relaxation. It's a technique to release any toxic or negative energy from your body. "

"No thanks, Jay." He says mimicking the soothing tone.

"It's Jason."

They have a brief pause and the therapy continues addressing Johnny.

Johnny talks about his fears, that after so many years of drinking, even sober he can't shake the feeling his wife is going to leave with the children. Her parents want her to leave him. He suspects another guy that she's 'friends' with is more than that. He can't blame her, he doesn't' know how to fix it. He's done so much damage.

Jason reassures him, "You must forgive yourself. You are a wonderful, kind man. Its building blocks of good deeds that will renew the relationship and she should appreciate your hard work. "

Jason is blatantly flattering him. He catches himself and redirects attention to Bill.

Bill whines, " I wish somebody took my wife, the emasculating bitch is on me about the garbage disposal again. Every time I say I'm going to fix something she hires somebody else. She doesn't trust me to do anything. Not my house, it's her way all the time. Who the fuck am I?"

Matt asks, "Do you know how to fix a garbage disposal?"

Bill answers grumpily, "No, no I don't."

Jason intervenes, " That's not the point, Matt. Bill is feeling emasculated."

Damien chimes in, "He's not feeling emasculated, he's not handy and she has to hire other people to fix shit because he doesn't have the balls to figure it out... or pay for it. He wants to take care of her? No, he's a fucking princess."

Matt giggles, "Exactly, he's a lazy bitch."

Jason "We don't use that language here. Now lets all calm down. Take a breath."

He addresses Peter. "You called me earlier this week, would you like to share?"

Peter admits to ordering a drink held up to lips. "I wanted to feel numb from this pain, but I stopped." He drops head in hands. "I'm garbage".

Matt raises his eyebrows.

Jason gently fills Matt in on Peter's backstory.

Matt laughs, "Seriously? Sorry, that's rough man."

"You're mean!" Peter shouts awkwardly, which makes Matt laugh harder.

Peter's voice gets higher pitched as he stressfully yells, "You can't judge me! You don't know me! It isn't right."

Matt "I'm sorry man. I just didn't expect that. You seem like a nice guy. Normal really. That's amazing, you're lucky you survived." He holds his hand to his forehead and bows slightly. He doesn't want to laugh again. The group bought it and they think he is crying and hiding his eyes.

Peter weeps. Jason has a box of tissues ready. Peter sloppily wipes his face and blows his nose.

Matt sits up straight, folds his arms and covers his mouth with one hand.

Peter begins his struggle with his attempts to find his birth mother. He had blood taken and submitted for matching DNA. No matches were found in the data- base. He researched online and even made a Facebook post about his search, a picture of him holding up a poster board with the date, time, and place of birth. Damien was playing with his phone that was constantly vibrating. It made him feel popular.

"Here it is." Damien held the phone with Peter's post proudly.

Peter was embarrassed. He continued in spite of his discomfort. "My parents, my adoptive parents, I mean, asked me to move out. They said my hoarding was 'unnerving' them. I'm thirty-six and I have a good job, but honestly I'm afraid to be alone I don't know if a rental will let me bring all my stuff."

"If it's garbage just throw it out. Maybe, they'll let you stay?" Johnny said and then caught what he said. "I mean, just keep what you need, what's important." Now he felt like he was making it worse. Eyes were on Johnny. " I'm sorry…"

Jason addresses the group, "This is a safe place. No judgment here. Anything said here, stays here. Matt, you are new to the group, would you care to tell us a little about yourself?"

"No thanks, Jay." Matt shakes his head.

"It is important to share, Matt. Everyone here needs to really know one another. There is a certain level of trust among the group that allows us to open up and grow." Jason hand gestures like a slow blooming flower.

"It's okay. I've got nothing Jay." Matt shakes his hand like he's jerking off gesture.

"Why do you think you are here, Matt?" Jason coaxes.

Matt says, "I think it's because somebody thinks I'm fucked up," he smiles warmly, "they might be right, Jay."

Jason has given up correcting Matt.

"Yes, well some of us have difficulty expressing ourselves. Do you trust Matt? If you want to observe, you're welcome to, but eventually you have to open up. It's only fair that each of you feel safe. Get to know one another." Jason droned in that ever so annoying gentle wind way.

Matt looks confidently at the circle of faces surrounding him. They can't be serious, he thinks to himself. Now aloud, "I thought this was like a lecture class. You know. You stand at the board and give a speech about feelings and how we should react in certain situations. Then we take a test and if we pass we go home with a certificate of completion. Like the driver's discount class from the DMV. Save on insurance."

Thomas chimes in, "A defensive driving course?"

"Exactly!" Matt throws Thomas a wide smile. Thomas feels smart and important, nodding in agreement with Matt.

Jason is startled that Matt doesn't even know why he's here. "No, Matt. This is therapy." He glances at the file. "May I share?"

"Sure." Matt responds confidently.

"You were remanded here by the courts for anger management? Is that right?"

"Yes, that is correct m—sir." Matt almost slipped and said ma'am but thought this bunch wouldn't see the humor in it.

"You shot a car?" Jason asks puzzled.

"Yes, sir."

"You don't have to call me sir, it's Jason."

"Okay, Jay."

"Jason."

"Yes, sir." Matt is enjoying visibly upsetting Jason.

"Where do you feel the anger in your body?" Jason re-crosses his legs.

"What? I don't." Now Matt was puzzled.

"Let's try this," Jason re-crosses his legs again, pursing his lips. "Tell us about your childhood."

It was getting late and Matt offered to share at the next meeting.

"Well, I am glad you are coming back, Matt."

"Let's stand for our closing meditation.", Jason states while rising.

"Christ you're fucking kidding me." Matt accidently says aloud. "I'm just not into that kind of thing."

"It's okay Matt. You will learn to love that quiet place of peace within yourself. Don't be afraid to just *try*."

They stand, hold hands, and recite a brief meditative prayer that Matt is not familiar with.

Matt has already sized up the group. Jason's gay and pretending to be straight, Peter's a good guy but he needs a backbone, Damien's a player with no boundaries and multiple obsessions, Bill's a spoiled douche-bag that cheats on his wife, Thomas's a clean cut rich boy that hasn't experienced the 'real world', and then there's Johnny, he's just a good guy. Matt didn't think he should be here in this land of misfit toys. Johnny has guilt, that's relatable.

Jason said, "Let's begin with Thomas. I know you didn't have a chance to speak about your situation last week."

Thomas describes the other nights fiasco that followed after yelling out his ex-wife's name during coitus.

Matt bursts out laughing. He raised his hand to high five Thomas. Thomas, taken aback, laughed too. The other members chuckle along with them.

"No, that's not funny. You know that Thomas." Jason says in a soft but snippy school teacher voice.

"It's kind of funny looking back at it now, Jason." Thomas defends himself.

"Yeah Jay." Matt backs him up.

Jason flips to a fresh page in his notebook and re-crosses his legs. With pursed lips he begins to question Matt on his willingness to participate this session.

Matt nods agreeably.

"Can you tell us about your childhood, Matt? It's the footing that builds ones character. It's a great way to begin the opening up process."

"About my childhood, Jay?" Matt puts his hand on his chest.

"Yes, take your time Matthew." Jason says concerned that he just passive-aggressively rebutted a patient.

Matt knew he had to give them something. He needed to pass the class. He could fail, but that was still no guarantee he'd get in the loony bin. That's where he wants to be, not this feelings crap.

"I grew up in a small town." Matt began as he reflects on the childhood memories he ran from.

A pretty white house with a wrap around porch on acres of land, the nearest neighbor is miles away.

"My father was the local Sheriff. The ladies loved him, including my mom. He was charming and because he was the local Sheriff. Power."

Matt is hanging out in town with his siblings. They see their father fucking another woman against a car in an alley next to the local bar. The brothers cover the sisters eyes but Sharon, Matt's favorite little sister pushed his hand away to watch.

Myra, a beautiful muscular black woman, walked by, pushing the stroller of their half-sister. Myra's eyes are wet with tears as she spies what the children see. She clears her throat and holds her shoulders straight. She was not the first and certainly not the last but she was the only one to proudly raise his bastard child. She never told anyone, yet everyone knew.

"You kids stay out of trouble, shoo. Go on your way."

"Yes, ma'am." They answered in unison and walked away in the opposite direction.

"My mother was a saint, people loved her dearly." Matt continued firmly.

Mother dressed in 1950's style even though it was the 1990's. She kept the house neat and clean, always the finest décor. She walked with an air, her chin up, commanding respect. She refused to believe the rumors and washed them away with a glass of red wine.

"It's good for the blood." she'd say.

She planned and prepared hearty meals each night from her well worn copy of Betty Crocker's Family Recipes. They gathered at the elongated finely refurbished mahogany stained reclaimed barn wood table set for ten. Hands were held before the main meal each night served promptly at six. Her at one end, his father at the other, she read aloud from the bible, it didn't matter what verse. She then thanked God for the bounty before them…in Jesus' name. " Amen."

"Amen." they all retorted in unison.

Then the frenzy of passed food and clattering of plates began. She stared at her husband in disgust as she sipped her wine, unaffected by the commotion.

"I loved her dearly. I was her favorite of the eight kids. I was the third boy."

When Matt is nine years old, Mother calls him to her bedroom. She is in a fancy silk negligee in powder blue with beaded pearls on the bodice. She puts down her glass next to the bible on her nightstand. She tenderly kisses his lips and whispers, "You're my favorite. You know that." She touches him tenderly. It excites him and the arousal grows between them. The memory fades to black in that sunlit room. She tells him, "You're a man now." He feels special and embarrassed at the same time.

"My dad kicked my ass a lot. He had to keep me in line. I was his least favorite."

Matt is seventeen in his mother's bedroom frantically pulling his pants up. His father kicks the door in and starts to beat Matt violently and slapping his mother around as she fights to hold his fathers arms back. She is sobbing. The physical fight continues until Matt is running out of the house. His father grabbed a shotgun from the fireplace mantle. Running. His father is shooting and cursing at him now.

Running. Running.

"So I left home at seventeen and joined the military."

Shots are fired. Matt is running in military attire. Running. Running.

"Then I retired and shot my neighbors car. So here I am." Matt concluded.

The story was bland but they all said they related to the father's rage and his mother's kindness.

"Was that after 9-11?" Damien asked.

Matt's annoyance is apparent. It's the question, always the same damn question. Is that important?

"No, it was in two thousand." Matt said flatly.

"What branch of the military?" Damien continued grilling.

Seriously? Matt thought to himself. He found this round of questions so routine they seemed trivial now.

"Marines."

Jason senses Matt's frustration and interrupts with an unexpected question, "Do you keep in touch with your family? Did they support your decision?"

"No, just my sister."

"How does that make you feel?" Jason paused, and then coaxed, "Lonely? Angry?"

Matt wasn't expecting a multiple-choice question, "Yes."

"Then you're in the right place, Matt." Jason said soothingly.

The weeks' pass and Matt has grown used to the routine of the weekly 'Men's Meeting'. He's now accustomed to their droning on about the same problems repeatedly. He notices people don't change very much, by nature. They are who they are. He realizes too, this is more of a venting session, a 'bitchfest', than anything else. He hopes he passes.. He complains about his boss and politics, though neither bothered him that much, he's fitting in. He thinks he's doing all right.

Summer is soon coming to an end. Bill was sweating steadily, beads soaked through his button down dress shirt. He was used to being overheated. Work required him to be covered from head to toe to protect himself from flying sparks, fumes, and debris. Today was cooler and his dress khakis and short sleeves should have brought him some relief.

Work, wife, his parents, all these obligations overwhelmed him. It wasn't them, he knew, but his internal voice wanted to blame, blame, blame.

Why are they making me do this?

He's a grown man now, but his childlike mind replayed his parents' failings. Memories of the red trimmed white gown, the bad breath of an old man, the heavy hand on his shoulder. His parents swelling with pride at the compliments doled out to them by Father Catano. The torn and tormented internal fight; instinctually he wanted to scream and hit this man who stole his manhood. There was nothing holy, nothing Godly about this man. His parents' nods and smiles subdued him.

They rarely smiled or had words of praise for him. Not for his long hours of study to keep up his grades. Not for the hours he spent aggressively performing as the best soccer player on his team. They never came to the games. Ever. The team usually lost, but the coach recognized his great effort and his natural talent. His parents heard the score and dropped interest immediately.

But here, in the Church vestry, they listened intently.

"What a fine boy!"

His rage would disappoint them. They attended mass every Sunday, were on the regular donation list, and recognized for their Godliness in the bulletin. What shame he would bring on them if he told the truth. So he kept it, the shame.

Today, they are renewing their wedding vows. Forty years. Not twenty-five or fifty but forty? Did they not think they would make it to fifty? They joked. They invited him back to his childhood church. He managed to avoid it all these years. He even stopped attending church altogether in his late teens.

Today was an event, a day to be recognized. They once again had to be the center of attention. Relatives are coming in from near and far for this spectacular feat.

Rebecca, had heard it all, had been through a rough life. He could tell her anything and she wouldn't bat an eyelash. She would have questions, though, so many questions. He wanted to answer and rehearsed the speech in his head. He felt stupid and inept, not able to find the words. He searched her face for a knowing.

She flipped her dark brown hair away from her pale pinkish face and gave him a stressed smile. She despised his parents and didn't want to go either. He knew that without any words of complaint.

"You okay?" she asked flatly.

"Yeah, just hot."

The drive, only forty minutes, seemed an eternity. He jacked up the air conditioning but nothing would slow the sweat that poured from his skin.

They smoked and listened to the radio. She asked questions, so many questions, he couldn't focus, so he ignored her.

"What's wrong?"

"Nothing. I don't really want to go."

"Me neither." Her voice was flat, calming.

Now sidetracked, he couldn't right it in his mind. The words eluded him.

Here he was driving to the Church, the church of his childhood, the church of alter boys in private 'sessions' and picnics and overnight beach "retreats". That's what they called them. He was too young to fight back but old enough to hide the shame. Time passed and somehow one day it was too late to fix. So he swallowed it and kept it deep down. He rubbed his hand on his distended belly where he kept it. It ached.

Was she still talking?

What the hell did she say?

"Answer me." She pleaded.

He didn't. He just wanted relief from this heat.

"It's not that hot. It's supposed to rain today." She attempted conversation.

What the fuck? He grumbled internally. Are we reduced to small talk, a chat about the weather?

Upon arrival at the Church, he was well aware that Father Catano was dead over five years now, but the smell of the church could not stop the sensory overload.

He smelled the hot breath that touched his neck. The place had not changed visually at all. The old pink carpet, high ceilings, tacky stained glass images of the crucifixion and temptations.

His parents greeted everyone excitedly at the rear of the Church. He put on his biggest smile as he shook hands, hugged and welcomed his kin. He looked in disgust at his wife as he made a few introductions. She never remembered their names. He didn't care but he feigned disappointment in her.

Now he had an excuse for his discomfort. It's her fault, she doesn't care about me, care enough to lose weight, care enough to know my distant relatives names, care enough to listen to me.

They all saw his sadness and reacted with dirty looks and eye rolls thrown in her direction. Why did she ruin things for him? They wondered.

She gently patted his damp back and whispered in his ear "I love you."

He gripped her hand tightly, almost cutting off circulation, as they sat in the pew. He would hold on to her for dear life, she was his rock. She's the only one who understands, even without words.

She sensed his pain. Maybe that was enough.

He wouldn't talk about it, today. After all it's his parents special day. "Look at them all welled up with pride." His belly ached. He was hungry and sick all at once.

The tears wouldn't come today.

Bill experiences guilt. He realizes he loves her and is suddenly fearful that he's going to lose Rebecca. He decides to share at the next 'Men's Meeting'.

The sunny haze of the hallway window always created an aura around Lisa's small dark frame. Her sharp short black hair with streak of another color each week, framed her round face with abrupt bangs. Her nose pierce glistened like a real diamond. Her room was diagonally across the hall from Matt's and they arrived home at the same time so often, he felt at ease in her presence. The thick black eyeliner made her dark brown eyes look wide and innocent.

He asked about her tattooed sleeves, "What made you want so many?" He gently took her pale arm in his hand and studied the contrast of skull's, koi fish, cursive quotes and cartoon characters.

"I never want to feel naked." Her eyes met his. Her lips colored in a dark purple that reminded him of licorice. The attraction was mutual. She pulled his hand, leading him into her humble but comfortable abode.

Working in the coffee shop left her smelling of flavors of syrupy sweet vanilla, coconut, and pumpkin spices. He touched her hair and pulled it just slightly to show his power. She let her head fall back and he kissed her neck with his whole mouth. Their hands ran smoothly as they pulled their hips in a grinding motion.

She pulls away seductively to light a jarred vanilla scented candle. "One." she whispers.

The room was colorful, a magical place compared to the dingy prison gray of his wall's. The make shift curtains made from bold colorful sari fabrics draped the small window. Her colorful bedding is unmade and looks inviting. Artificial flowers propped out of recycled bottles with the labels peeled off. The lights are dim because she covers the lamps in scarves.

They lie sweaty and peaceful in the narrow double bed after the passionate and successful orgasms are exchanged. He heard under her breath that she was counting reps. He didn't mind it intrigued him. She stroked his chest with her short polished nails, black with zebra stripes and hearts on the ring fingers.

"I like your nails."

"Thank you, I just get the two done with a design." she admires them, " Two."

He kisses her hand and asks about the pile of books on her dresser.

"I take night classes at Nassau Community College. I'm going to be an accountant. I have a thing for numbers.", she answers confidently.

He noticed her tapping his chest now in patterns of three repeatedly. He didn't mind. She felt good. Everything wet about her, felt good.

"Three." she whispered.

The weeks pass by and their trysts are a regular pattern now. Matt blows out the candle and slips out when she is asleep to return to his own bed down the hall. He studies her sweet obsession with numbers. Lisa counts things. Almost everything, steps to cross the room, ice cubes in a glass, even the number of times they make love. She never wears sexy underwear, she is comfortable in her body and dresses casually in every layer.

Her thick black eyeliner can't mask her sweet innocence. They talk about music and touch each other's tattoos, never asking the stories behind them. It's comfortable.

He asked about her family once, she joked, "Why? Do you want to meet them and we can talk about our escapades over dinner. 'Pass the buns, speaking of buns...'", she giggles at her own joke.

"Seriously, I want to know about your family. Why are you here?" Matt faced her on his side of the bed and his large hand brushed wisps of hair from her damp face.

"I don't have a family. I don't want to talk about it." Lisa pulled the blanket tight to her chin. Her eyes grew heavy and sad. "I'm sleepy." Matt tucked the blanket around her and kissed her forehead. She smiled with her eyes closed.

He absorbs this oasis. He never feels hurried or rushed in Lisa's room.

One early evening, he was fumbling with his key and a bag filled with artificial flowers he picked up for Lisa at the dollar store. He asked the clerk to wrap it in a ribbon. Her door opened, Matt turned with a wide smile. A young man, much closer to her age is kissing her goodbye, promising to call, they laugh. The young fellow is dressed in a black band t-shirt matching Lisa's over sized one, but he has jeans on. Their thin crossed arms reveal the matching blended sleeves are scars of understanding.

A world Matt missed. A world Matt had never known.

Matt enters his room but leaves the door ajar. After the goodbyes, Lisa came down the hall on her tip-toes and peeks coyly in Matt's room.

"It's not like we are…"she began.

"I know." Matt emptied his pockets onto his dresser, not looking in her direction.

"I'm sorry, it's just…"she tries again.

"Lisa…"

"Yes?"

"I…" he had no words. His heart ached. Is this love? He wondered to himself. I don't like this part. "You don't know me." He looked at her directly, "You just know the idea of me." The words came out painfully.

"Oh." she stared a moment, sadly, waiting for him to touch her, reprimand her, she longed for him to do something! She spotted the variety of fake colorful flowers peeking out of the black plastic bag he dropped in the doorway. She leaned on the doorjamb. Matt did nothing, just stared at the dresser and the contents that had spilled from his pockets.

"Okay." Lisa returned to her room sullen. She counts her steps. "Eleven." he heard her say.

Matt listened to the heavy door click and latch. It was over. Just like that. He closed his door and lay on the navy blue comforter on the twin bed of his sparse room.

Matt put on his headphones, listening to *Jeff Buckley's* version of *Hallelujah*. One tear fell. Just the one, "One." He counted.

It was Wednesday night, 'Men's Meeting', he had something to say.

The months have passed swiftly. The meetings were productive. They took turns beating throw pillows with a padded bat to release anger, while yelling at past demons. They spoke their *truths*, and shared their shame, confidences, insecurities, regrets, and the 'ones' that got away. Yet, being *sensitive men*, they were guarded and never revealed the root causes of their suffering. It was easier to blame than take responsibility.

They gather and start to settle in the small room. Thomas enters rushed and panicky he is sweating and pale. He tugs lightly on Johnny's arm and pulls him to the side of the room. Johnny smells the liquor on Thomas's breath. The smell is coming from his sweaty skin as well. He's obviously taken up drinking again.

"You're drinking again Thomas." Johnny asks.

"Yes. Yes. Johnny that's not the problem though." he's visibly shaken. " I need to speak with you privately after the meeting. I need you. It's really…really important."

"Sure Thomas, no problem." Johnny nods and adds, "Don't sit next to Jason."

"Of course, of course. Thanks, Johnny."

Johnny is sad. He doesn't even want to be here tonight and now he will be out later. He just wants to be home with Annie. He's not paying attention tonight as he daydreams about the happy and simple dinner conversation earlier this evening. He can't help smile a little when the image of a small food fight broke out and he had to pull peas from Annie's hair.

Thomas picks the seat next to Matt. Matt smells the alcohol immediately. He turns to grin at Thomas, noticing his trebling hands.

"You alright Thomas?"

"Yes. Yes. Why? Yes." He stirs in the seat and stills himself. Confident cocky Thomas is a mess, Matt takes note. Matt leans back, arms folded and legs out-stretched and crossed at the ankles.

Jason gestures with arms wide that the room is open. "Does anyone have a pressing issue that they need to share?"

Bill's face is red with beads of sweat. He raises his hand slightly to get Jason's attention. He shares his feelings of confusion that boarders on love and hate in his constant daily dealings with his wife, Rebecca. He thinks he loves her and feels inadequate. He doesn't know how to love.

Jason is gathering his thoughts a moment. He wants to use the right words for defining 'marital love'.

"Marital love is a complexity of variables. We don't feel the same way every day. That would be dull. That's just not love. There should be open communication and an under-lying trust. Do you feel you can communicate honestly and trust Rebecca?"

"BUZZZZ!" Matt makes a loud buzzer noise, "Wrong answer Jay."

Matt redirects his attention to Bill, "Did you fix the garbage disposal yet?"

"No." Bill grumbles.

"Well than you suck."

"Matthew! No, that is not appropriate!" Jason raised his voice. It was masculine this time.

"Are you emasculating me Jay?" Matt asks in a childlike manner.

"What? No Matt." Jason is annoyed and defensive.

"What the fuck do you know Matt? Years she's been torturing me that I'm not good enough for her. Her late husband was sooo won – der – ful." Bill barks.

"Are you?" Matt asks, his hands clasped leaning forward facing Bill.

Bill red with rage, "No, but I could be if she just, just,…"

"Yes." Matt waits.

"She's a fat fucking spoiled bitch, but I love her."

"Okay. Maybe you should take her out, walk her or something?" Matt states flatly.

"Like a dog?" Bill chuckles as he asks. All of them laugh now. All except Peter. He's lost on marital jokes.

"Not to interrupt you Bill, you do need time and space to process your complex feelings. Maybe we could spend more time on that in our private session. Agreed?"

"Agreed." Bill looks somber but Jason is the only one he's shared his extramarital affairs with. Now might not be an appropriate time.

Jason doesn't like Matt taking over the focus of the group. He re-crosses his legs and turns toward Matt.

"Matt, I got your message earlier. I'm very sorry to hear about your breakup."

"Thanks. It hurts so much. I didn't realize how much Lisa meant to me these past few months. She's all I looked forward to." Matt chest grows heavy and he sobs, dropping his face into his hands. The tissue box is passed to him. Lifting his head to rest on his fists he cries, speaking slowly between sobs, "Today my heart is broken. Completely broken. That's never happened to me before."

Jason asks, "Where he feels it in his body?"

"In my heart Jay, my heart." The tears subside as Matt focuses on the stupidity of Jason's question.

Damien raises his hand. "I think we're in the same boat Matt." Damien goes on to express his fears that his fiancé, Faith, is not attracted to him anymore. Their long distance relationship is failing. The more he travels, calls, and texts the more she pulls away. The last trip he stayed for almost a week and she made excuses, they didn't have sex at all. Damien was feeling rejected and lonely. He spent hours sexting other women, going to the gym, hitting on women there, and out to nightclubs with friends and hitting on more women. "They love me, I'm charming, but they can't fill that void. I don't screw around with any of them. I just want her. If she's not going to put out, it's over. I'm a man. I have needs. I have fantasies to fulfill."

Bill whispers to Damien, "I know how to handle that."

"Huh?" Damien looks confused.

"We'll talk about it later."

Jason wanted to hear more about the fantasies but the more appropriate question came out, " Do you think you just want someone you can't have? That you desire the unattainable because you know it will fail? That some part of you deserves failure? Rejection?"

Damien's mouth is open and he has a realization. That's exactly the problem. He shares this light of wisdom, "My mother said so many times, you're charming, but if anyone gets to know the 'real' you, they won't love you!" Rather than cry, he sits with this, "Undeserving."

Jason eases the blow, "You are undeserving of such harsh words, such harsh judgment from your mother. The one who should love you unconditionally?"

Bill is ready to leave his wife. He openly admits to the group that he has a girlfriend on the side. "What choice did I have? She neglected my needs!"

"You don't have sex either?" Damien asks.

"No, she takes care of my sexual needs, no problem there, it's everything else. I've always had girlfriends on the side. It's my nature. It's who I am. She just isn't enough or she's too much. I don't know."

Jason nods fervently," I fully understand Bill, your inability to connect with her. She's a tough woman, Bill."

The meeting ends with a soothing meditation. Matt admits to himself that this is working, he feels a lot better than he did just a few hours ago.

Fall has arrived. The guys talk outside, in smaller groups. The cool night is windy and quite brisk. The leaves on the trees are changing color, the sky is dark gray with cloud cover. They are exchanging numbers and decide to meet at a local diner to keep talking.

Soft music plays in the background. 'I Wanna Get Better' by the Bleachers is on.

Damien flirts with the waitress, "Hey, I really like your outfit, Jolanta." He read the nametag pinned tightly to her ample bosom. "It really accentuates your curves." , flashing her his charming smile.

"Thanks sweetie." Jolanta says with a wink.

Damien is not aware he's obnoxious.

"How you doing, baby?" Jolanta turns her attention to Bill. She squeezes Bill's shoulder and strokes her hand down his arm as she rounds the table taking orders.

"I'm alright." Bill answers in his deepest voice with a slight Italian accent. He flushes red as he eyes her over. "How you doing?"

"I'm so good." She responds. Bill chuckles.

Thomas is annoyed with her presence. She needs to hurry. When she walks away Thomas says, "She's just another Polish whore looking for a green card husband."

"Oh. Oh. Whoa Thomas! You can't say that!" they all chime. Bill is the most defensive.

"Seriously? It's the truth. They're all over the city and dating websites. They're always looking for some loser to fall for them. They're all syrupy sweet until they hook the poor bastard, then turn into bitches once they get what they want. It's a game."

They stare at Thomas. They can't argue.

Peter thinks about this as a dating option.

Johnny is quietly sharing suspicions of his wife's cheating, which is heavy on his mind.

Thomas, his voice shaking now, interrupts Johnny impatiently. "I've got a problem with my car, Johnny." Thomas is sweating profusely. He needs a favor from Johnny. Thomas explains in a panicky voice that his car was in an accident.

"Just go through insurance. You've got the money?" Johnny retorts annoyed.

"No. I can't report it. I don't know what happened. There was blood and hair on the front fender in the morning. Johnny you have to do the repair on the low down."

"You mean the down low?" Damien mocks Thomas's lack of street knowledge.

"I'm sorry, Damien, I don't speak niggerish." Thomas snapped.

"Whoa, whoa, ohhh" they all chime in again, correcting Thomas's faux pas.

"You can't say that Thomas." Damien shakes his head.

"Easy Thomas. That's not how we speak here." Johnny mocks Jason's voice. They all laugh at the unexpected humor coming from quiet Johnny.

Bill asks Thomas, "Were they black pubish looking hairs in the grill?" Laughter breaks out again. Peter doesn't understand the joke.

Matt gets their attention by clearing a throaty cough into his hand. "Look I know how all of us can get what we really want." He had them. "But in my experience, it takes discipline and self control. If you have a clear objective, have a strategy, follow the plan and conquer." He spoke firmly and concisely.

Bill wants his wife dead – hates her – insults her – justifies his cheating because girlfriend sends a sweet text. It is the waitress in the diner.

"How?" Damien asked.

"Look Damien, you're the loose nut in this wheel, so I'm warning you now, don't open your mouth to anyone! Understand?" Matt was grinning as he spoke.

"I don't even know what you're talking about." Damien was puzzled.

"Peter you hate being alone because you believe it's all you deserve. I have a perfect woman for you but you need to upgrade your status. That's Thomas' job. Get him a quick 'in' in real estate, a new look, and a better attitude. I can provide all the documents; fake certificates, licenses, I.D., whatever he needs."

"You can do that?" Peter asks excitedly.

"Yes. No more questions." Matt puts his hand up to hush them.

"He works for you, Thomas. Teach him how to schmooze and dress for success. Damien will hit on Johnny's wife to see her reaction. So Johnny, you'll have your answer either way."

Johnny nods in agreement and then Damien does the same.

" Damien you want your fiancé jealous and your sexual desires fulfilled, well your sitting right next to the best instructor." They all turn to look at Thomas. "No you numb nuts. Bill." They look toward Bill. His face flushes red.

"How do you know?" Bill asks Matt with a coy half smile.

"I know your type. I'm familiar with the Aye Aye program. Can you get Damien in?"

"What's that?" Damien addresses Bill.

Matt answers, " It's an adult sex club, where Damien can live out his sexual desires without commitment. Isn't that what you really want?"

Damien nods.

"Bill?"

"Sure, no problem." Bill is proud and puffs out his chest.

"Thomas you need your car repaired without a record? Johnny can you handle that?"

"Well, I'll have to bring it in the shop at night initially but once I start, I can get it done." Johnny has done this before for relatives. He shrugs it off, "No problem."

"What do you get out of this Matt?"

"Peter's got to buy me a new car." He pauses, "I really need a car. I'm sick of driving a suspicious white work van, with tinted windows." They all laugh uneasily. "Don't worry Peter it won't break your bank account. I want a 2009

70

Chevy Malibu. Had the highest rating that year and it's *inconspicuous*. I think that's a fair price for a good woman." he smiles.

"What if she doesn't like me?" Peter sulks.

"Jesus, Thomas, you've got your work cut out for you with this one." Matt rolls his eye. They all laugh. He has them hooked.

"What about me? What do I get out of all of this?" Bill huffs.

"I'm going to kill your wife." Matt states flatly. Their eyes are fixed on each other.

They are with him until shocked by his last suggestion. They mull it over quietly. They don't sincerely feel bad. They've been listening to Bill's complaints for over three years now. They are more concerned with getting caught. How's he going to do it?

"I'm not going to get caught. If I do, it's on me." Matt knows what he's doing.

Still they look at each other with uncertainty.

"I can make it look like an accidental overdose. Slip and fall. "Dizzy on the stairs" after her surgery. You're not home Bill. Understand?"

"I'm in." Bill crosses his fat hands across his distended belly and leans back with a half grin on his face. He's happy.

They all agree.

CHAPTER 17 – THE GAME BEGINS

Thomas made a few calls Thursday and the 'new' used car was ready for Matt to pick up Friday morning. Matt admired its ambivalence. Nothing special about it, a silvery gray interior and exterior, low mileage, and economic gas consumption made it a perfect choice.

Friday evening Matt is set to observe Bill's wife, earlier that day he set up 'bugs' in the house. He sits in his car around the corner while eating a deli sandwich. His ear buds hooked into his laptop give him a glimpse into their private life. He hears conversations, and arguments. She's right and he realizes she is not the bitch Bill painted at all. Bill is just a sleaze and a liar. But Matt feels obligated to keep up his end of the game. He turns the car on occasionally for warmth, with the radio on low playing '*Try Again' by Aaliyah*.

Peter *'accidentally'* meets Sharon at a charity function for orphans, where he is recognized for his substantial contribution. He is an act, suit and tie, new haircut and manicured nails. His new career equipped with business cards and the impressive BMW he rents as a business expense are all meant to impress.

Peter woos her with great ease. He starts to believe the story, and thinks this is who he 'really' is or he should have been if not discarded. He isn't giving up the role. He became a very successful upscale real estate agent, is excellent at the job, a natural salesman. His income increased swiftly.

They dance and flirt. ***Imagine Dragons 'Radioactive'*** sets the mood. The night has taken them swiftly into a passionate frenzy. He sleeps with Sharon. It was easy. He starts to think in the afterglow, that maybe he's too good for her. He stays with her anyway, because Sharon never wants to talk about family. This makes him feel safe.

Damien keeps picturing Johnny's wife. He's obsessed with her sweet ways. His fiancé, Faith, is growing more suspicious and jealous. It's working, he has her attention but now he wants Annie. On the way to meet up with Bill, Damien posted happy pictures and posts of him and Faith. She would see them before she went to bed and miss him, feeling loved.

The Aye Aye meeting was a joke in reference to Friday night at the sex den. Bill would tell his wife he had to go to an AA meeting whenever he needed a fix. Bill couldn't believe the other guys never heard of it. It made him feel superior and he confidently led Damien in the entrance of the blackened window bar.

A chalkboard sign marked Aye Aye Night sat just outside the cubicle entrance. He held his chin up giving a 'what's up' head bob to the doorman/bouncer. The music played the usual stripper club rhythm that aroused the crowd and titillated the senses. ***DJ Snake and Lil John 'Turn Down for What'*** blares from the speakers. He led the way through the almost blackened room. In a slow motion they maneuvered through the crowd. Backlights of pinks and blues revealed glimpses that the flurry of sexual activity had already begun. Eyes were on them as they moved their bulky bodies through the waves of erotic dancing women.

Damien was startled when a hot blond in heels and a thong approached him, her face was wrinkled and sour when the white spiral of light scanned the room. Maybe, this was not such a great idea, but Bill kept walking towards the back and Damien followed him to an open couched booth awaiting them with a low table to set their drinks.

The use of condoms was promoted here and there were bowls of an array of sizes and variety of flavors. Damien in his obsessive manner had calmly studied the options and chose a few to try out. They were horny, not stupid.

The naked, other than a mesh skirt, waitress took their order they doubled down on drinks of coke and lemon. They didn't drink, that made them classy compared to the dirty drunks in the bar.

Damien recognized the waitress immediately when she rubbed Bill's shoulder the way she had in the diner.

"How you doing, baby?" She flirted leaning her breasts into his face. He laughed that side smile of his. Then lashed his fat tongue out and licked her nipple and then after showing its girth swallowed a mouthful of her breast. She held his head tightly to her and paused before stepping away to get the first round.

"That's my girl." Bill stated proudly to Damien, "For now. She likes it in the ass. I can never get my wife to get into that one. A man's got to do what he's got to do."

Bill leaned in to explain over the loud music. In a serious businesslike manner he informed Damien how this all worked. It was free. You're not doing anything wrong. It's not like prostitution. They want it, like you want it. Just find what you like and go with it.

"Like Peter, he's always complaining he can't get any. He can have it all! Go for it Damien. You're single. It's guilt free. You want anal, I know plenty here that love it. They are begging for it, Damien."

Damien was flush with embarrassment and excitement. He scanned the room, so many bodies. The base of the music intensified his erection. "Do you feel guilt Bill? You're married."

"Nope. This is like, family tradition. You provide at home, but what you do on the side is just for entertainment. Fantasy."

"But you don't provide?" Damien never held back opinion.

"I'm there, if she needs me. She just never needs me. Hell, I don't even know if she cares if I dropped dead." Bill shook off any sense of guilt.

Damien just nodded in agreement. He could see why she thinks Bill is a selfish man. Damien checked his phone repeatedly as it vibrated. Faith 'liked' the picture of them at a ball game taken last weekend. Cute.

Bill started taking off his clothes down to his boxers, his fat belly hung over but did not distract from the fact that he was indeed well endowed. Damien followed suit and a few women, a mix of young twenty to forty something year olds, began gyrating around them. The ladies were all getting a little drunk with drink and passion. Before long, Damien and Bill were in orgy mode with the rest of the buzzed crowd. *'We're Up All Night' by Daft Punk* is playing.

Johnny picks up Thomas's 2015 Mercedes from his private garage in the city. Thomas, of course has a rental, the same make and model, so as not to draw suspicion.

It's petty badly damaged but definitely drivable. He takes the keys from Thomas and enjoys the ride, the smell of fine leather, the smooth way it handles the bends in the Belt parkway and then the southern state. The heated seat and steering wheel are comforting in the chilly night. Johnny puts the radio on. He leans back enjoying *John Mellancamp's 'Peaceful World'*. He likes this taste of luxury. It's a far cry from his 2007 Nissan Pathfinder.

Johnny stops at a twenty-four hour self help car wash a few towns away from the body shop and cleans off as much of the evidence. He wonders if this is all worth it. Then he wonders what could have possibly happened to some innocent person that he was washing away the memory of. He hadn't heard anything on the news but he rarely watched the news. That was Annie's thing, she liked to be informed and would give him the highlights of headlines and weather reports. He worked so hard, physically. His asshole boss was demanding and in the evenings when the television was on Johnny dozed right off to sleep.

Johnny opened up the shop in the industrial park. He was surprised at the amount of activity this time of night. He flipped the lights on, pulled the car in, then closed the garage door from peering eyes and got to work.

Time had passed. Winter had come. Rebecca had her surgery.

The plan was simple. Bill would put an extra dose of oxycodone in Rebecca's food. Then she would take her usual dose. She would return to bed exhausted. Bill would meet his brother at the boat. Bill would text shortly after he left, she would answer, she always did. She didn't want him to worry.

Hence the alibi, "She was alive when I left."

Matt would enter the unlocked, unalarmed backdoor, sneak upstairs to the bedroom and, without struggle, he would throw Rebecca's limp body down the stairs. If she still showed signs of life, Matt would snap her neck. It's a simple case of slip and fall after over medicating herself.

The children would come home and find her lying there. The police would be called. Bill would be called. He'd rush home and feign tragic shock. The tears would flow as he fought past the police begging to hold her "one last time."

He grinned as he prepared the breakfast of scramble eggs laced with crushed percocett and diazapam. He played a compilation of Barry Manilow songs on You Tube in the background. He was in his 'happy place' mood.

Matt looked up the address in advance and committed the directions to memory. He was covering his tracks. He changed his license plates over to a set he found in a recycle pail months ago.

He parked around the corner from Bill's wife's house. Bill's truck was still parked out front. He should've been gone by now. Matt was agitated, one does not diverge from the plans of attack. He slipped the lanyard I.D. tag around his neck and grabbed his clipboard. He tucked the polo shirt into his pressed khakis and tightened the black baseball cap with matching logo of a security company. He walked up to the front door and faked ringing the bell for appearances. Matt wondered if Bill had changed his mind. Through the glass front door, Bill waved his arm signaling for Matt to enter the side gate. Matt walked confidently through the snow to open the side gate and enter the back yard. The gate was jammed with snow and he had to push repeatedly to get it to open wide enough for him to slip through. He realized Rebecca was right that Bill was lazy. He didn't even clear a path for the murder he planned.

Matt tipped his cap and headed to the back of the house and sat quietly under the awning by the kitchen windows next to a sloppily stacked pile of wood.

"Hey." Rebecca's voice startled Bill.

"Hey." He stood at the kitchen counter sorting the pills into the little blue boxes labeled by day of the week.

"What are you doing?"

"Just organizing your pain meds. I'm headed out to meet my brother. Problem with the boat…" He rambled on using technical terms.

She let the pugs outside. Rebecca was used to this routine, all day long, dogs out, dogs in, dogs out…

The sliding doors opened and closed and he heard the murmurs of an ongoing conversation. The pugs didn't notice Matt at first they had to do their business. Once the fat one noticed him, they both approached and were yapping at him aggressively.

He mouthed a silent hush, but found petting them calmed them swiftly. He pet one then the other, scratching behind their ears as their little piggy tails wagged happily. They shook the snow off their tiny cold bodies and headed back into the house.

Rebecca let the pugs back inside. They were always starved for attention and she had to be careful with them following her so closely under foot.

This time Rebecca shut the screen door but the sliding glass door she left ajar to let in the fresh cool air.

"I'm getting claustrophobic from being house bound so long." she said in an agitated tone.

Bill wasn't much of a talker, so the longer the explanation the bigger the lie. When he said "going to work on the boat" during the off season, it really meant he was out to meet his girlfriend. Bill thought she was fooled, that he was a man's man and maybe this time he was meeting his brother. She didn't care anymore, she tried to love him, but the years of his perpetual poison lies had taken its toll.

He sorted the meds. He swapped out the RX Ibuprofen half doses for the real Percocet this time. He sadistically enjoyed watching Rebecca suffer. He liked the need, the begging for comfort in her tearful brown eyes. That sweet sadness was what first attracted him to her, well that and the money. He enjoyed her pain, he had a need to be needed. How dare she question him! He was her savior.

The foot surgery had taken its toll on her. She was unable to shower and her hair was greasy from the soaked sweating of pain. Today she would wash it over the sink. She made it up and down the stairs on her buttocks and had to be cautious not to slip on the ugly pale pink bathrobe covered in red hearts. Everything was a chore, a painful process, and she was angry. Her patience had worn bare thin.

Is he still talking? She wondered why his line of bullshit carried on so long today.

"I thought you promised to fix the garbage disposal today?" She snapped.

"I did." He said flatly. She didn't believe him. She scraped the breakfast he'd so carefully prepared for her into the sink, ran the water, and turned the handle.

"There." He said proudly. "It worked."

She was happy. "You did it." She raised her hand to high five. He didn't move. She rubbed his back and watched the water run smoothly as the grinding sound stopped. "It's finally working."

"You just threw away the food I made." His face was red with rage. She chuckled. She just didn't care. She was relieved the garbage disposal worked again.

"I'll make you another." His expression was sullen but his eyes sparkled. He readied the pan, eggs and spices. He fumbled as he sorted the pills. It was intentional so he could slip some away to be crushed and added to the new meal.

"Why do you always lie to me?" She said taking a seat at the counter and sorting through the mail that had piled up for days.

"I can't deal with your crazy shit! Why do you always accuse me? I don't know what you're talking about!"

"Yes you do." She said flatly.

He started his stomping around the kitchen, phase of the argument. She knew the drill. Yell, stomp, storm out. It was all too familiar. He cooked swiftly this time and shoved the plate in front of her.

Matt could clearly hear the escalating argument. Matt was growing more agitated with Bill's erratic behavior. Neighbors could hear raised voices. Matt was increasingly uncomfortable with Bill's plot falling apart before him. "Bill is an asshole, she's right." Matt muttered to himself as he tightened his black uniform jacket and rubbed his eyes in annoyance.

"Eat up. You have to keep up your strength." She eyed the plate and the bottles of pills. She hopped around the counter and grabbed today's first dose. Something looked different but she didn't know why. She took the pill and drank water directly from the tap, wiping what spilled on her face with her sleeve. She just didn't care any more.

He was ranting now. Grabbing his wallet, his keys to the truck she'd bought him, his phone that she paid for. The phone chimed. He looked at it nervously. His face turned red. He was embarrassed that he was mid-rant about his faithfulness as his girlfriend texted another kissy face, "See you soon". She would meet him at the boat too.

"Give me the god damn phone!" Rebecca held her hand out. She was firm as she held her one footed balance against the kitchen counter.

"You're fucking crazy! It's my brother, I'm late." He turned his back to her, as he placed the phone in his pocket.

Rebecca opened the fridge. Next to it shone Bill's collection of specialty kitchen knives. He had two sets and a butcher style sharpener. He loved cooking, he loved eating, and he loved cutting up his 'kills' whether it be fish or deer meat. Of course he spent her money on 'the best of the best' in butcher quality steel kitchenware.

"Is he still defending himself? Yes." She thought to herself. She knew the guiltier he was, the longer the rant.

"Shut the fuck up." Rang in her head. She pulled the largest knife in the collection from the butcher-block holder and held it close to her side.

"I know honey." She said as the long sleeves of the oversized robe draped past her hands.

She put weight on the injured foot and hobbled uneasily towards him.

He turned facing her now, smiling. "Look at you! You're doing so much better."

He opened his arms wide to hug her. She placed her left hand on his shoulder. He smiled.

"I'm getting away with this!" he thought to himself. "She's such a fool." He leaned in for a kiss.

She never swayed from eye contact and plunged the knife with all her might into his heart. All his weight fell forward onto her knocking them both to the floor. She screamed in agonizing pain as his leg crushed her bandaged foot. She pushed and shifted his dead weight off of her. He landed arms wide on his back. He weakly grabbed at her as the blood spattered from his chest.

"You fucking loser. You think I'm stupid? You think I don't know?"

His mouth opened to plead his innocence but just blood came out. It made a gurgling sound much like the garbage disposal. His arms fell to the floor and his blue eyes fixed a permanent gaze.

She withdrew the knife from his chest and found a comfortable position on his belly then continued to stab at him fervently.

"Yeah, I'll fix the garbage disposal. Five fucking months! Yeah, I love you, fucking liar. Yeah, I'll take care of the yard. You hired a fucking landscaper then gave me the bill you fucking loser. Yeah, I love you babe, No, no you don't you fucking piece of shit. Yeah, I'll take care of you, No, you got to fix a fucking boat, or kill a deer, or fuck a whore, or go fishing, or see a fucking therapist and complain about your daddy and mommy, or go to AA, or hang with your friends. I'll take you out – oh maybe? Fucking maybe? You say I'm too fat, you're embarrassed to be seen with me, look at you, you fat fuck! I hate you, I hate you, I hate you…" Rebecca felt better now as the tears and blood spilled.

Bill was unrecognizable at this point, just a lump of fatty meat. She stood up and hopped but the blood made the ceramic floor slip on her knees. She pulled herself up to the counter and retrieved what looked like a small ax to chop up the dear meat. She crawled on her knees back to his body. **Copa Cabana** blared on the computer in the background. She hated that song.

"And I hate Barry fucking Manilow!"

She searches her I-Tunes account on the computer for *The Rolling Stones* *'Gimme Shelter'*, and she blasts it full volume on a loop.

She began the arduous task of dismembering his body. Chopping him up unprofessionally. She was not a cook. She grabbed random pieces and put them in the sink. She ran the disposal and let the water keep running.

"Well, look at that, it works." She giggled.

She continued but it would jam on bones, so she set them aside on the floor. The pugs licked his face and their fur was getting matted with blood. The blood on their faces made them look ferocious. They shook the excess from their little paws, they didn't like to get wet.

They picked up the little bone pieces and carried them around. She was afraid they would choke. "No, no outside boys." She let them out the back sliding doors and they scampered across the yard leaving little red paw prints behind them in the snow.

Matt heard everything.

She is shoving pieces of Bill in the disposal and running it, "What's that, I can't hear you?"

"Oh Shit!" Matt laughed. "Good for her" he whispered to himself.

The pugs are out again.

"Shit." Matt jumped to his feet as the bloody ferocious faces are barking at him wildly now. Matt grabbed a piece of firewood waving it to keep them back. He can't have any traces of blood on him.

The grinding motor of the garbage disposal and Rebecca's voice echoed in the crisp air of the suburban garden. Matt slips out the gate closing the latch tightly. Cap still tilted over his eyes and clipboard tucked under his arm he walks swiftly back to the car.

A school bus pulls up just as he started the car. The red stop sign folds out and he is blocked in as the children exit happily in colorful winter attire. They are stomping in the slush and snow with heavy backpacks in tow. The group separates in the different directions headed to the warm welcome of their homes. Rebecca's children look serene but serious. They had experience beyond their pink faced years. Here, awaiting them would be just another. "They'll be okay." Matt muttered, "I turned out okay. They'll be okay."

The bus pulled away. Matt followed. The radio played 'If you like pena coladas and getting caught in the rain...'

Time had passed and she had gotten nowhere it seemed at the task of disposing of him. "You're so fat. There is so much of you. Disposal's jammed up again."

He didn't respond.

She grabbed paper towels to sop up the blood. "More work. Thanks Bill. Now I have to clean it all up."

The front door opened. Her children were home. The house alarm is set off when they enter.

"Mom?"

"Oh hi guys. How was your day?" "Mom?" they look at the bloody chopped pieces of their stepfather.

She smiles "Don't worry, I'll clean it up. We're probably ordering out for dinner. I just got to get this god damn garbage disposal to work."

"Mom?"

The son leads the younger daughter out and they run. She shuts the alarm and the door and gets back to work. Still yelling at Bill.

When the police arrive, Rebecca is sitting in the back yard on a rocking patio chair next to the fire pit. It is overflowing with piles of wood and bone, Bill's head propped sideways on top. The police have guns drawn and her glassy brown eyes look at them nonchalantly. She looks back at his head and tilts hers so their eyes meet.

"Goodbye." Rebecca says softly.

'Gimme Shelter' by the Rolling Stones is still playing through the sliding glass door.

The News 12 van films her being taken out of the back yard with her matted knotty hair hangs over the shoulders of the bloody robe. Through the open gate, other officers are seen with hands on hips watching the fire and gray smoke warm the crisp winter afternoon.

News report: Rebecca pleads guilty by reason of insanity and is remanded to the New York State Utica Psychiatric Center.

The 'men's group' including the therapist, Jason, attended the wake.

It was a closed casket.

Damien started up a conversation with Bill's brother about boating.

None of Rebecca's family was in attendance.

It is a short and quiet wake. Coworkers and distant relatives came. A few whispers, "I always knew she was crazy." buzzed about the small room.

His parents sat stoic, unmoved, but expelled a few crocodile tears here and there for dramatic effect. It was dull, like Bill.

No one really knew him.

The girl from the diner came in uniform with her nametag still intact. Jolanta seemed the most distraught and was confused by the lack of emotion. She sat quietly in the back.

She thought, "I am the whore that caused all this." She had waited at the boat docks for almost two hours with his brother, Michael. Taken by Michael's equally masculine and direct personality, she swooned and slept with him. Was it revenge this time for Bill not showing? Or was she just that desperate for attention. It wasn't the first time with Michael. He was just as good and an easier catch because he's not married. But she had chosen Bill, he had more money, a green card wasn't enough.

Michael looked her way and gave a wink but wouldn't acknowledge her directly. She would meet up with him again, that made her feel better. She carefully wiped her face, wet with tears and snot. She stood hands on her back to stretch a moment. Her baby bump was showing. The DNA doesn't matter. They are brothers after all. It could be either one of theirs. Jolanta was set.

Offering his hand, Jason, paid his condolences and introduced himself as Bill's therapist.

Bill's father, enraged, pulled him in close, "Get the fuck out before I kill you with my bare hands."

Jason left so swiftly he didn't realize his effeminate gait that he reserved for nightclubs and 'special' moments, was so prominent.

Matt saw it. "He's a gay." He whispered to Johnny.

"What?"

"Nothing."

Following the cue, Matt, Johnny, Thomas, and Peter left separately. Damien stayed and flirted with Bill's cousins.

Peter was finally somebody. Thomas had pulled strings and created a new man out of nothing. Peter didn't see it that way any more. Thomas may have given him a break, an identity, but Peter was succeeding. He learned the business and was a successful real estate broker. He had spent his whole life not knowing who he was, but this was the real him. He knew to his core. He was a natural schmoozing customer's, flipping contracts, and making contacts. Money was rolling in faster than he could count. Peter cut off communication with his adoptive family. He didn't them anymore. They were a constant reminder of his past.

Not only had Peters identification changed and he became abrasive and arrogant. Peter passed Jack on his way to visit his old coworkers at the bar.

Jack shouted to him and reached up to shake his hand.

"No more free lunches." Peter pulled away so as not to dirty his new Armani suit and rolled his eyes at filthy Jack.

"Long time no see Peter. I take it you found a good woman?" Jacks smile broadened as he held his hand still up to gesture a handshake. "I understand." He dropped his hand into his lap.

Jack recited "Jack be nimble, Jack be quick, Jack be a simple man, but at least he's not a DICK."

Peter cringed and stopped for a moment, his back to Jack. He stood taller, took a breath and walked over to his keyless entry BMW. *'Classic Man' by Jidanna,* smoothly flows from cars state of the art sound system. He doesn't miss the key collection.

Jason, soppy and tearful, passes around a box of tissues. "So, so, incredibly sad. This has been..." he gasps slightly, "such a difficult tragic experience for all of us. I feel within this space, everyone should be free to express themselves. Bill will truly be missed."

Silence.

"No judgments here." Jason states warmly.

Damien is crying and balances the box of tissues on his lap.

"What're you gonna jerk off?" Matt jokes. Damien doesn't respond.

Peter announces he got another promotion.

"Well that's great Peter but that's not exactly what I meant. I was opening the room up to share our feelings about the loss of our dear friend, Bill."

"Well, it's kind of related." Peter states. The men grow uneasy in their seats.

"How?" Jason asks with his head tilted like a curious puppy.

"I got to thinking about him dying so suddenly and all that, well, we only live once."

Jason interrupts, "So it brought up feelings of your own mortality. That's good Peter, go on."

"Well, I'm seeing this girl and she can be a real bitch sometimes. I just want to strangle her. Just shut her up. I see that now, that sometimes a woman can hurt and destroy you. I don't want to be 'that guy' like what happened to Bill, immature."

Jason, "You mean emasculated."

Matt is containing his rage, though his face is flushed red. Thomas throws a sideways glance to Matt and rolls his eyes. He shakes his head and drops them in his hands.

Peter continues, "Yeah, that. I've been building myself and working so hard to be a better person, to be 'somebody'. Sharon's taking me for granted. She doesn't appreciate me."

Jason confirms Peter's feelings, "Yes, Peter, it may be time to move up, move on, move away from that kind of negativity."

Thomas can't stand it anymore. "What...the...fuck are you talking about? You're a fucking loser!"

Jason intervenes, "Now, Thomas, *language.*" He says almost singing, "We don't use those words against each other. This is a safe place."

Johnny giggles remembering the imitation he did of Jason at the diner.

Matt leans forward staring deep into Jason's eyes, "How you made it a safe place for Bill to be a lying, cheating, bastard to his wife and it got him killed. Yeah, good call Jay."

"It's Jason, and I can not be blamed for that, his wife was obviously crazy.", Jason states smugly

"Whatever."

"I'm not so sure about that." Matt's gaze still fixed on Jason.

"Did you not listen to the news? You attended the wake."

Matt leans back in his chair, "Yeah, and?"

Jason says in a high and mighty tone, "You're obviously having strong hostile feelings about this Matt. Were you ever married? Do you even have a woman in your life?"

Matt snaps, "What the fuck does that have to do with any of this? He's dumping my sister because he thinks he's too good for her. He's lost his mind!"

Jason turns to Peter, "Wait, What? You know his sister?"

"Sharon is your sister?" Peter is suddenly afraid of Matt. "She's a lovely girl..." he stammered, "Just not my type."

"Type?" Thomas jumps out of his chair and begins pacing the small room. "Type?" louder now. "Peter you think you're so high and mighty! Not your type? You're nothing. Is that a type? You came from garbage and garbage you'll always be."

Peter puts his chin up, "I don't know what you're talking about?"

Jason intervenes, "Now, we don't do that here. Let's calm down."

Thomas still raging, "Then what are we doing here Jay? We're supposed to be getting to the truth. Finding our truth, isn't that what you say? Well the truth hurts. Peter's not even in the truth. He's delusional! Sharon's in love with the fantasy I...I...I—"

"We." Matt interrupts.

"Thank you, Matt, *we* created!"

"Peter can you explain what Thomas is saying? How that makes you feel?" Jason is confused.

"No." Peter won't make eye contact with anyone.

Jason asks Thomas, "You know Peter's fiancé?"

"Not directly." Thomas says calmly.

"Please sit down, Thomas." Jason gestures to the empty chair.

Thomas reluctantly sits.

Damien has been playing with his phone and only half listening to the outburst. "Sharon's hot." He holds up the bikini picture of her on his phone. He had been scrolling the pictures on her Facebook page. He just friended her while they were talking. Without thinking first, the words, "Johnny's wife is hotter though." fell from his lips.

Johnny charged him and knocked him backwards to the floor, his adrenaline pumped through his body as he smashed Damien's pretty boy face repeatedly. At first no one responded and just let it happen, immune to rage.

"Stop them! Stop them!" Jason yelled like a woman waving his hands flamboyantly.

They pulled them apart and coaxed each other reassuringly back to their seats. The circle was heavy with hostility.

"So Damien, how do you know Johnny's wife?" Jason asked in a jealous tone. He wanted baby Damien for his own.

Johnny answers, "I saw the texts Damien."

Damien is cocky and proud, "So you know she wants me." He flashes his charming grin.

"You text his wife?" Jason is annoyed now.

Johnny jumps out of his seat to pummel Damien again but this time Thomas and Matt hold him back. "Calm down Johnny boy." Matt said with a grin.

"What'd you call me?"

"I don't know." Matt and Johnny get the giggles and sit down.

Jason "Let's all take a breath. Lets all calm down. I sense a lot of tension tonight. Death can bring that out in people".

Matt laughs. They all become quiet for a long pause.

Matt asks if they all want to go to the diner after the meeting.

"Fuck you." They answer in unison. Except Jason, he pouts that they go out together without him.

Matt wants to clear the air with Damien.

When approached Damien calls Matt "A crazy mother fucker."

"Bad call." Matt says under his breath.

Matt is daydreaming about Lisa. Even though she lived eleven steps away, they had grown miles apart. They didn't even pass each other in the hall anymore. He puts the radio on to distract his own thoughts. *'I Wanna Get Better' by the Bleachers* gripped him as he sang along loudly.

Damien always liked a challenge. The more Johnny's wife, Annie, pushed him away the more he wanted her. His mother's rejection of him all those years had taken its toll and the price was craving rejection. She was dead many years from a brain tumor taking her life swiftly, but her voice still rang in his ears whispers and shouts of worthlessness.

Once he proved to Johnny that Annie wasn't looking elsewhere for attention he should've stopped pursuing her, but he didn't. He wanted her now. She wasn't even his type, hadn't seen the inside of a gym since she was a teenager but he was becoming obsessed with Annie's sweet gentle ways and he continued to send little texts.

"Hi."

"Hey."

"How are you?"

"I miss you."

"I care about you."

Sometimes she ignored it, and considered blocking him, but there was a sense of flattery in his attempts for attention. She'd answer occasionally, but coyly insist he should stop. It isn't right.

Annie had started to stand a little taller and smile more often. Secret schoolgirl giddiness filled her. The little things like putting on make-up and styling her hair before heading out to run errands with or without the children, had taken prominence over housework. Once a week her mom would take the kids so she could get things done that were impossible with them under foot. Sometimes she used the day to catch up on much needed sleep, clean up, or get her nails done.

With the knowledge that Annie was a devoted wife, Johnny came home on her 'free' day during his lunch break and found her standing in front of the wall mirror in their bedroom trying on a new pair of tight black pants and a cute bosom flattering top. She moved flirtily, flipping her hair with her hands on her hips. She made a seductive pose. The clock radio played loudly on the nightstand and she didn't hear him come in. He leaned against the wall in the hallway.

He loved her curves, the few extra pounds she gained worked on her, he thought to himself. He knew that wasn't something to say aloud. It never came out right, any comment about Annie's weight would lead to a fight. He watched her bend over to stuff green garbage bags with old worn out or stained clothes along with the old maternity attire that had been a staple in her wardrobe long past pregnancy.

"Hey sexy." He called to her.

She was startled and blushed. "How long have you been there?" She giggled and flushed with embarrassment.

"You're beautiful." He walked towards her slowly. "Don't be shy with me. "

Ed Sheeran's 'Thinking out Loud' played on the pop station.

His hands around her waist now, she looked down at the sorted bags: one garbage, one donate, and clothes strewn across the room and unmade bed to try on.

Looking up at him now, Annie saw love, nothing but love. So much had gone wrong in the past. She was guarded, afraid of the unpredictable. This moment though, her heart was heavy with love, only love. His eyes had a longing, his touch was strong and tender. He pulled her closer to him know. They swayed to the music and he kissed her forehead, her neck, stroked her hair. They were against the bed now and climbed into it. His body on top of hers, a passion they thought was lost, coming to life in them again. Stronger now.

The buzz of her cell phone somewhere in the pile of tangled sheets and clothes, Damien said "Hi."

They paused to find the phone just in case it was her mom calling about the kids.

TEXT from 'Stacey'.

Annie tossed the phone aside. "Not important."

Johnny knew the code from Damien. He had told him she hid his number in her phone under 'Stacey'.

Johnny pulled away and sat silently on the edge of the bed. His mind was racing, what was going on? Was it all a lie? She was involved with Damien now? The hair, makeup, clothes? Was it all for him?

"What's wrong?" Annie wrapped him from behind letting her hair fall on his shoulders and gently wrapped her arms around his chest.

"I've got to get back to work." The sadness came over him and turned to anger. Why is Damien still texting her? Secrets and lies, he wasn't imagining it this time. He hated this game. She wasn't going to tell him. He had no words.

"I love you." Annie squeezed him.

"I love you too." A gentle kiss and he dressed quickly. He was sweating, here it comes, the anxiety. His heart raced he felt the throb of blood in his ears.

When she heard the front door close, Annie read the text and immediately deleted it. She wouldn't answer, this time.

Johnny rushed to work slamming the dashboard with his fist, as *Mr. Brightside by Killers* blared, his heart raced. He wanted a drink to take the edge off. Instead he parked in a quiet parking lot, soaked with sweat now, he ripped his jacket off and screamed. A lady carrying a small pile of books from the library skid on the ice, startled by his outburst.

He called Damien to confront him, but the call was rejected and went to voicemail.

"What the fuck is going on? " He sat a moment awaiting a response, then realized there wouldn't be and hung up.

He apologized and offered to help her to her car. "No, no, no thank you." She was visibly frightened.

He laughed and shook off the cold. Pulled himself together. He would confront Damien later.

At the counselor, Jason's advice that they communicate and support each other outside of the meetings, he called Matt and vented. Matt always had a calming way about him and he took in the details and reassured Johnny that it was probably just a test.

"Did she answer?"

"No. I don't know."

"Then it's all good, Johnny." Matt knew this was a lie, but he needed Johnny. He needed Johnny sane.

"What if she texts him now? I'm not there."

"She won't Johnny, Damien's a moron. Annie's smarter than that. She already turned him down. It was just a test. She loves you Johnny." Matt said it monotone and Matter of fact. Johnny was oddly soothed by it. It started snowing again. The white began to cover the gray slush and dirty snow mounds about the lot. Fresh snow always made things seem clean again.

"Everything will be alright, Johnny." Matt's voice surprised Johnny. He had gotten lost in a daze and forgot he was still on the phone.

"Thanks Matt. Really, thanks, Matt."

"See you tomorrow, Johnny."

Damien was waiting on the other end of the phone. He continued texting. He asked Annie if she could send another sexy selfie. She liked that, he thought.

His phone rang instead. It was Johnny. Reject call. He'd listen to the voicemail later. This could be trouble. For some reason, this made him hornier. He scrolled his saved pictures. He stared at the one of Annie in a bra and panties from last week. She didn't make a pouty face like the young or immature women he collected. They thought that looked sexy, they looked stupid like fish faces, he thought.

Annie, was different, she had a nervous smile and her arm hid her belly, as her hair hung over an eye and dropped to her shoulders as if she were hiding some secret place inside herself.

"That's hot." He responded and promised to delete it. He never would. He scrolled through his collection of scantily clad women that he'd met and coaxed into sharing with him. He felt better. Then he felt sad. None of them loved him. None.

He texted Annie again, "Would you like to meet me for lunch on my sail boat? It's winter, so it's docked. But I'd really like to see you, spend quiet time alone together. Please say yes. I miss you."

Annie was angry Johnny walked out at such an intimate moment. He was distant again.

She opened Damien's text.

"Yes." was all she said.

CHAPTER 24 - SAILING

Matt had just finished reviewing the texts between Annie and Damien. He stepped out of the warmth of his heated vehicle and headed across the park toward the docks.

Matt stood on the crisp snow under a leaf bare tree strewn with icicles. Winter had been brutal. He looked at the partially frozen sound of north shore long island sound beach. A few boats were still docked. Damien's was one of them.

It was time to "shelter in place". The storm of Damien would be here shortly.

Matt stood watch, taking in the view. The heavy gray looming gray clouds meant another snowfall would blanket the shoveled pathways and shrubbery of the small beach park. An afternoon train broke the frozen silence of the ritzy North Shore town. Summers were active and lively but winters stagnant and lonely.

'The dead of winter.' Were the words that danced in Matt's head. He snickered.

The lights were on in the distant mini mansions that speckled the hills surrounding the bay. Dark gray smoke and the smell of fresh burning wood escaped the chimneys and left a warm homey scent against the back drop of white and gray death.

Matt had hand warmers in his gloves and boots and squeezed his extremities to feel the heat. His steel blue eyes peered out between the flipped up the collar of his gray wool pea coat and gray knit hat tight around his ears to block the wind, covered most of his face.

It was time. He watched as Damien's jeep pulled up. He brought the good car to impress Annie. Their afternoon tryst on the sailboat wouldn't be Damien's first go round with a conquest. He was prepared with spare blankets and snacks. The cold worked to Damien's advantage, he was prepared with the offer of body heat and they'd long for his strong warm hands and hot breath on their skin. He knew what women wanted, physically, and he played the game of charming their pants off, figuratively and literally.

Damien spotted Matt, a few yards away, the only person standing in this field of white blending in with the cluster of gray and black trees. The snow began to fall. Vanity prevented Damien from pulling on a hat. He didn't like the way a tight hat wasn't flattering around his big head. It made his face look fat.

He approached Matt, annoyed at the interruption. He was in a hurry to ready the boat but at the same time happy to see a familiar face. It made him feel special, popular.

"Hey." He busted out his charming smile.

"Hey." Matt smiled warmly.

"What are you doing up here?" Damien wondered.

"Just enjoying the view."

"Are you spying on me?"

"Now, why would I do that, Damien?"

"It's just weird. Do you live around here?"

"No, but you've painted such a pretty picture of this place, I thought I'd come and check it out for myself."

Damien was concerned.

"Can I check out the boat?" Matt asked.

"Now's not a good time Matt, I have plans. Got a lot to do today. Got to work on the boat and put some chains on my old truck tires…." His words trailed off.

Damien noticed Matt wasn't listening. "I've got to go Matt. Enjoy the view. You really shouldn't stay out here in the cold and all though. You might get frost bite."

Matt takes up the offer to see the boat, even though there wasn't one.

In the sessions, Damien had bragged about his attachment to the boat and his many conquests, now it was time to show it off. His broad chest bloated up with pride and arrogance.

"Have you ever been on a boat before, Matt? Do you sail?"

"Yes and no."

"What do you mean?"

"Yes I've been on a boat but I've never sailed." Matt has a brief flashback to his time in the military where the troops were transported by ship in the gulf.

He remembered it was dark and the sounds of sea and vomiting comrades he had to clean up after. No, he didn't like boats.

They passed a small office building by the dock. A light was on and a radio playing was barely audible. Two cars were parked by the entryway but all blinds were closed to keep out the cool draft.

"No work today Matt?"

"I've got work. Just have to take care of some things first. Get things in order."

They carefully stepped down the icy plank stairs and walked the docks, treading carefully to the third slip. There it was, Damien's pride and joy. They climbed aboard as Damien chatted on about technical difficulties and repairs to be done in the spring. Damien continued to reflect on the memories of spreading his mother's ashes in the bay, and his eyes teared up.

Matt was unsure if this was from the cold or if Damien was actually having a sentimental moment. If it was, it was one he practiced often, it sounded rehearsed. Maybe this was an act he used on his lady friends to make him appear sensitive and they would comfort him.

"I thought your mother was a bitch? Why would you want to sail with her?" Matt asked flatly.

"How could you say that? I loved my mother. She was a wonderful woman." He paused. "She didn't love me though, I was never enough."

"Are you?"

"Am I what?"

"Enough?"

"She always said I was charming." Damien chuckled and smiled widely.

"Is that enough?"

Damien's phone chimed. He pulled it from his pocket as they entered the cabin but he didn't read it and threw it face down on the bed. He was afraid it was Annie and didn't want Matt to see it.

As Damien fumbled to put the heat on, Matt studied the cabin. The bed already made with an assortment of blankets and pillows was inviting. The large boat, enough to sleep four people, had a kitchenette and bath shower combo.

"Coffee?" Damien offered.

"No thanks."

After scanning the cabin, Matt stepped out onto the deck. He noticed an assortment of tools loosely wrapped in a blue tarp. Matt grabbed a rusted gaff and studied it in his hands.

Damien followed and stood behind Matt but faced the parking lot for signs of Annie's arrival in the navy blue mini van. He's told her to park next to his jeep. He was relieved she hadn't shown yet.

"Maybe you'll be with her soon." Matt said.

"Who?" Damien was puzzled. Did Matt know about Annie?

"Your mother."

"Oh. Yeah." Damien's hot breath made a cloud of white in the already hazy gray of the bay.

Matt swung the gaff plunging it into Damien's leg, then pushed knocking Damien off his footing and he flipped backwards head first into the freezing waters. Damien's feet kicked violently. Matt Wouldn't let go of the gaff until the kicking ceased. Matt watched the blood float up in the bubbles of air.

When Matt freed the gaff, Damien's face came upright with eyes wide, still under water he grabbed worthlessly at the side of the smoothly polished boat. His blue eyes fixed on Matt's. Damien sank into the murky water.

"Say 'hi' to your mom." Matt giggled.

Matt got to work staging the tools and tarp to appear that Damien was working and it was a tragic accident. This wasn't Matt's first go round.

Matt went back into the cabin and read the text. It was from Annie.

He read the message from Annie coded as Ann. Damien, for all his bragging about being a technology expert for FDNY and FEMA, was not that bright.

"I can't do it. I'm sorry. I love my husband. I can't do this. You're a really sweet guy but I can't. Sorry. Take care of yourself."

"Good girl Annie." Matt said.

He forwarded the message to Johnny from Damien. "See Johnny it was just a test. Annie loves you!"

Johnny texted back, "Thanks Damien."

Matt sent one more text to Peter from Damien's phone.

Matt downloaded Damien's entire history via 'the cloud' to his own laptop. Then left the phone face down, as it was, on the bed.

Matt thought to himself, the I-phone gloves were such a great invention. He wished he had thought of it, would have made a fortune.

He looked over the deck, checking on Damien once more. He was gone.

Matt popped open the back of the jeep and took the duffle bag containing Damien's bunker gear.

Matt carried it as he carefully stepped back to his car, barely visible in the flurry of snow that fell. He drove a few miles through hilly side streets until he found an area to pull over by a wooded lot. He popped the trunk, grabbed a screwdriver and license plates and began the task of reattaching them to his vehicle.

He spotted a few drops of Damien's blood on his pea coat and retrieved a jug of holy water from the back seat. He soaked a rag with the icy chucks of blessed water, then he blotted the small drops, reciting the 'Our Father' until they were clean.

He was clean.

He put the radio on an oldies station *'Sailing by Christopher Cross'* played smoothly as he rounded the winding roads.

When Damien's father and fiancé were called into the morgue for identification purposes they both remarked through tears how fat his head looked. His frozen blue eyes bulged from his huge face. It was definitely him.

Matt grabs Damien's duffle bag of bunker gear from the trunk and catches the train to Penn Station. He heads to The Majestic at 115 Central Park West in Lincoln Square, New York City where Peter now lives with Sharon.

Matt texts Thomas to meet him in the lobby at four p.m..

Matt is dressed as a service repairman. The long sleeved t-shirt prominently displays an elevator repair company logo. He puts a yellow construction helmet on a block prior and keeps his eyes down to avoid the cameras.

In the basement, Matt uses his laptop to link up and control the electrical system. He immediately transfers the information to his phone. He stops and strikes up a conversation in the doorway of the security office. A bored man working the security cameras in the room takes to chatting to break up the monotony of his day.

Matt texts Peter that he needs to "meet him in the lobby. They need to discuss something important." He watches the camera screens until he notices Peter in the hallway of his floor heading to the elevator. He is with Sharon.

Peter texts, "On my way."

"Got to go. Duty calls." Matt smiles at the security technician.

"Take care man."

Matt slips into the bathroom and changes covers his clothes with the bunker gear and swaps out Bill's work helmet for Damien's firefighter helmet. He stops the elevator between the third and fourth floors through his phone. He removes an ax from the duffle bag and heads up the stairwell racing to the third floor. Using the ax he pries open the elevator doors on the third floor.

It's four o'clock.

Inside he hears Sharon and Peter frantically press the emergency buttons and a familiar voice from security informed them the FDNY would be there shortly. The security man is using a walkie-talkie to ask other staff if they have seen the elevator repairman around the building? He was just here a few minutes ago.

Sharon is nervously complaining about the inconvenience and inefficiency of the old building. Peter complains in agreement, in his new uppity tone he mastered.

Matt keeps his head tilted down and takes out his phone.

"It's fine sir, you may exit now."

"Are you kidding me? I'm not crawling on my new Armani coat like a squatter. It cost almost two thousand dollars. We'll wait until it's repaired."

Sharon still annoyed, "We have to go Peter. Nicky and Dino are having the opening. We can't be late again, and I need at least two drinks in me before it starts. Those two are insufferable sober."

"You always need two drinks in you." Peter voices arrogantly, meaning to embarrass her.

"What? That's not true at all." She folds her arms in a huff and leans against the mirrored wall of the elevator, checking her hair and make up once again. She tilts her chin up, perfect.

"This happens all the time sir. The power is down. Just step through sir." Matt reaches his free, gloved hand into the open gape without looking up.

"Oh, man up Peter!" Sharon snaps.

Peter on all fours puts his head and arm through the space, feeling claustrophobic but wanting to get away from her. Matt holds his arm and presses the power on button on his phone restoring the power to the elevator. The doors swiftly slam shut, the motion sensor was over ridden and the elevator drops to the floor crushing Peter's head. It was not as bloody as it was loud. The crunch of bones, Peters one arm snapped backwards and knocked Matt slightly off his footing. Matt let go.

Sharon's screams could be heard throughout the building.

Matt grabs his gear and heads to the stairwell.

Thomas was waiting in the lobby. There is no sign of Peter. He approaches the reception desk to ask if there is a message for him.

The Fire Department truck shows up and the black and yellow bunker gear of fire fighters spills into the ornate marble and Chrystal chandeliered lobby. Matt crosses the lobby and leaves through the tall glass doors. Thomas is looking around confused. Matt holds his hand up slightly and bows his head to avoid Thomas. Matt walks out and turns down the first corner. He slips into an alley way changing his clothes swiftly and dumping the gear he had loaded with

Thomas's DNA, a comb, a book of matches, and old tissue, before realizing a homeless man is sitting quietly observing him while sipping from a Starbuck's cup.

"Shhh." Matt held a finger to his lips.

The homeless man blinked unfazed. Matt threw him a small roll of one dollar bills wrapped in a rubber-band he'd kept hidden in his boot.

"God bless you." The man muttered.

Matt walked tall back into the business of the streets and hailed a taxi to Penn Station.

Thomas is waiting and watching growing impatient in the lobby. Two firefighters are bringing a woman off another elevator. She is sobbing but enjoying all the attention. She feigns fainting and leans onto a large leather backed sofa.

Thomas watches as the elevator doors open again and a black body bag is wheeled out on a gurney out into the sunshine that blared through the tall glass windowed doors. A haze shown in the streams of light and the world seemed to be in slow motion. Like he was watching a soul being carried to the pathway into the light.

Sharon wails again. Thomas realizes it is Peter.

Thomas turns back to the reception desk to question the clerk. His eye catches the overhead camera eyeballing him.

"Never mind." He rushes out to the street. No sign of Matt anywhere in this mass of black.

In the taxi, Matt, pulled a jug of the holy water from his duffle bag. He poured some on his boots. He splashed his face and hands as he rocked back and forth reciting the 'Our Father'.

"What are you doing sir? You can not make a mess in my car." The driver stammered between his thick Pakistani accent and obvious stuttering implement.

"It's my prayer time." He lifted to show the driver held his hands in prayer.

"Oh." The driver paused. He was agitated by the traffic, he was not an aggressive driver and kept getting cut off. He just waved his arm in frustration so as not to disturb Matt's praying.

The FDNY was able to extricate Peter's body from the elevator but left the NYPD with two crimes to solve:

1)   Why was Damien at the scene on the video? It wasn't even his firehouse and he wasn't working that day.

2)   Who was Peter? Sharon behaved hysterically, understandably, but none of what she told them about Peter or the identification he carried were real.

They were going to call in his boss for questioning

The commute on the train back to suburban life was crowded yet peaceful. The smooth rattling of the rails lulled Matt into a reflective state of mind. He felt pangs of guilt. All he wanted to do was take care of Sharon. He remembered her as a little girl and how they would play in the fields surrounding their childhood home. They would do anything on a dare and found solace in the stunts and pranks they carried out. She sang curse words and started fires, and was often punished for behavior unbecoming of a young girl. She was a grown woman now but he had to protect her from the evil men in the world. Peter was a good man, he thought, he was the chosen one. Matt thought his suffering would make him appreciate all the qualities she possessed. Peter had taken on 'the role' and sadly fell from grace.

Matt didn't know all the details of what happened after he left home all those years ago, but he'd heard bits and pieces of rumors, and collected news clippings from his small hometown.

As Matt ran, his father, in a rage continued to beat his mother and the children in his path. Two of his older brothers intervened and wrestled the shotgun from his hand. They warned their father, it's been said, they warned him, the shots were fired, an ambulance was called but it was too late.

Sharon and the other girls wrapped around his mother slumped in a corner, sobbing, all of them. His mother asked for a drink and her bible, they obliged. They sat around the traditionally decorated living room as she shared the soothing words of Psalms.

A week later they found her cold limp body gripping that same bible in her bed. She lay on her side, one arm draped off the side where the bourbon stained the rug spilling from the sparkling Waterford Crystal tumbler. The diazepam the doctor prescribed to ease her nerves wasn't enough, he guessed. Accidental overdose was what he heard. The papers kindly printed 'devoted wife and loving mother died in her sleep'.

The children separated into groups. The elder ones caring for the younger, was all worked out. Sharon, considered the 'wild child', was sent to live with a distant relative in New York. They took pity on her and taught her the ways of the world. City life suited her. She was always entertained and could roam for hours with veracity.

Their childhood home was a hard sell. The insurance paid out swiftly on the Sheriff's death. His mothers insurance, deemed it a suicide, and did not pay. The parents' excessive child rearing, excessive spending habits, wanting the best of the best to keep up appearances had a price, the years of accumulated bills took most of what they received.

No one wanted to stay there. It wasn't a home anymore. No one wanted to buy it. Word was all about the small county, a murder-suicide home was an evil place surely haunted by nightmares, if not ghosts. The once whitewashed and polished home, had once appeared in 'Country Living' magazine, was now left abandoned became dilapidated and was sold for a small fee to a builder, who knocked it down. Any signs of its existence were in glossy photos and memory.

Matt wondered who took the photos, the jewelry, and the polished furnishings. Who went through all the clothes, the letters, and the attic full of holiday décor.

No one knew why his father went mad that frightful day. His temper and bad behavior would catch up with his father one day. Everyone knew that. The inquest found his brother that pulled the trigger "not guilty' for the reason of self defense. They never spoke of the reason behind the madness. His mother, so angelic, such a good woman, would rather die than live without her favorite son, so she died.

Sharon was the second to youngest girl and by far Matt's favorite. He taught her card games and let her win sometimes. He brought her presents of chocolate covered junior mints for which she was always wide-eyed and grateful.

When Matt spotted Sharon in last years issue of a New York Life magazine toasting at a charity gala, her hair and frame had changed but nothing, not even time and misfortune took away her smile or the sweet innocence of her wide-eyes.

He owed her something, he felt. Finding her a good man, a good adoring husband would be his penance. When he heard Peter's story, Matt thought a lost soul like him would understand and treat her kindly. Peter needed to just raise his status to be able to give her all that she deserved. The education, the change of wardrobe, and identity, all worked. He was a worthy man.

Matt was angry now. Why did Peter have to complain about her at the 'Men's Meeting'? Why did he judge her so harshly? He was garbage after all. Peter believed his own façade and that he was too good for her. Jason supported Peter's thought process. Matt was angry now, enraged.

Peter *had* to be eliminated. Sharon could not suffer the rejection. Matt hadn't known she would witness it, that he regretted. Her screams of horror echoed in his head. It wasn't right. Jason should have stopped Peter, put him in his place. Peter didn't understand that women are a gift from God. He disrespected her. He disrespected God.

Matt had pangs of guilt and the holy water wasn't enough to wash away his pain this time. He braved the icy roads and carefully pulled into the church parking lot. He silenced the radio and blew his hot breath on his cold numb hands as he rocked back and forth repeatedly reciting the 'Our Father'.

He rang the rectory bell and requested to speak with Father Giovanni. He was asked if he had an appointment. Puzzled by the question he just stared at the heavy set middle aged woman.

She asked again.

"No." he dismissed the question.

She suggested he have a seat while she checked if he was available.

"No thank you." Matt loomed over her desk as she called Father Giovanni's extension. She was unsure if she should press the panic button. Luckily he was available and would be out to greet him shortly.

They stared at each other. Her discomfort was palatable. She offered him coffee.

"No thank you."

The ticking of the second hand on the clock seemed louder in the quiet. She continued her tedious paperwork trying not to make eye contact over her thick and tilted reading glasses. The silence made a disease in the formal traditional style office.

She jumped in her seat when the phone rang.

Matt giggled under his breath. She eye rolled at him and the tension was broken.

Father Giovanni was in plain black dress with a heavy sweater cut so high in the neck it barely revealed his official white centered black collar.
Handshakes and introductions were made before Father recognized the tall handsome man from the vestibule font.

"Come in, come in Matt."

Father led him down a narrow hallway to a neatly decorated office. Books shelved with various comfort reading materials grief, loss, addictions, marital advice. A large scrollwork metal cross hung high behind his desk. The angle of the sun coming through the blinds made its ridges sparkled and there was a glowing smoky effect around Fathers head and shoulders creating a halo aura effect.

This comforted Matt.

"How are you Matt?"

"I need absolution Father."

"Yes, feel free to speak."

"I've killed people." Matt dropped his face in his hands.

Father Giovanni felt for this poor veteran on a deep personal level. He too had suffered tragedies of war when he served in Vietnam and although so many years had passed, sometimes he was still haunted by night sweats and flashbacks.

The withdrawals from opiates upon his return to the states, the rejection of his family and old friends, until he had found solace in Jesus, he suffered.

"I understand Matt, more than you know."

Matt, wide eyed, believed him.

Father Giovanni continued, "There is evil in this world. People are capable of horrific acts and sometimes it is our responsibility, no, our duty to do things that go against our beliefs and convictions, it shakes our moral core. Yes, even taking a life, because it is in this Truth...for the greater good. It's hard to comprehend that we are spiritual beings having a human experience..." he lost his train of thought.

Matt exhaled aloud. He thought Father went a little Oprah Winfrey on him there, but he listened anyway.

"I know it's hard to put into words but I don't think you should relive the experience, punishing yourself for eradicating evil. We have to protect the world. The truth is, sometimes it's ugly, horrific really but we must protect the innocent, the meek, and often the only option is to take the lives of those that are a violent, selfish, imminent threat, because they are driven by evil."

Matt leaned forward, Father did understand, he knew these kind of men and the means and reasons for their demise.

"We have to destroy the evil doers, even though it pains us, to save others. Matt, from great pain and suffering."

Father Giovanni paused and studied Matt's features. His words had definitely impacted him. The furrowed brow and the heaviness in his face had relaxed. His eyes glassy with tears and his lips drew half a smile. Matt leaned back dropped his arms on the rests of this suddenly comfortable chair.

"I seek absolution. I want to confess." Matt stated his claim.

Father Giovanni was aware that it is unhealthy for PTSD patients to relive the experience. "No need for details, my son. Do you feel in your heart that God loves you and understands your suffering? Your sorrow? Your remorse?"

"Yes." Matt knew that he longed for Gods grace. "Yes I do."

"Then we will begin." Father Giovanni stood beside Matt, held his hand over his head as the ritual of absolution began.

"God the Father of mercies, through the death and resurrection of your son, you have reconciled the world to yourself and sent the Holy Spirit among us for the forgiveness of sins. Through the ministry of the church, may God grant you pardon and peace. And I absolve you of your sins, in the name of the Father, and of the Son and of the Holy Spirit. Amen."

"Amen."

Father Giovanni directed Matt to go in to the Church and light a candle for each person he killed and say the Our Father after each lighting. This would serve as his penance.

In the Church Matt knelt before the idol of Mother Mary. He pulled a bunch of singles from his wallet. He pulled from his boot a thick pack of ones in a roll with a rubber band around it. Some were stained with blood. There was a small sign with 'Suggested Donation $1per candle.' He found irony in this, one life, one dollar.

He inserted the first dollar and tried to remember his first kill. He honestly couldn't recall a face, was it covered? He definitely didn't know a name. The process began pressing the little red button that lit an electric flame. "Our Father……"

He continued until he entered Peter's name and lit one more for good measure, maybe he forgot someone. He wasn't sure anymore.

Father Giovanni going about his evening ritual of locking up the church braved the evening wind in the dark on the icy trek from the rectory to the large entry doors of the vestibule. He shook his cold hands and rubbed them together as he blew his hot breath on them.

He drew open the grand double doors from the vestibule into the church. The wind whipped down the aisle and a flurry of dollar bills floated gently like feathers about the tall church. The church was glowing. Not only had every electric candle been lit, hundreds more lined the aisle, the altar, and sat in pews.

Father Giovanni stood in awe at the beauty and the destitution of it. Motionless, his chest grew heavy with the weight of what it represented. Tears rolled down his cheeks, he wept on choked gasps.

The wake was filled with an abundance of people. Family, of course, many women he had befriended over the years and a huge turnout from the FDNY.

"Such a tragedy."

"He loved that boat."

"So young, what a shame."

Much pomp and circumstance, as his fellow firefighters took turns standing honor guard. His father was pleased with the turnout, a lot of hand shaking and kind words exchanged.

"Truly will be missed."

Matt, Johnny, Thomas and Jason made calls and sent texts. Jason didn't feel it was appropriate that he show. Being his therapist, it wasn't protocol. The others decided to meet at the evening service.

Matt, Johnny and Thomas entered together. They waited on the long line to pay respects.

Matt and Johnny approached and knelt by the casket.

"He looks so fat." Johnny said.

Matt held back a laugh.

"His head is so big."

"Stop." Matt whispered in a giggle.

"He was going to fuck my wife. She was crying in front of the T.V. What the fuck?"

"Sorry Johnny."

Johnny started to weep. Matt patted his back to comfort him.

"Fucking glad he's dead."

"I know Johnny, it's all going to be okay."

They stood up and shook hands with Damien's father and fiancé, feigning condolences. Faith, Damien's bleach blonde competitive body builder girlfriend seemed masculine and stoic, even though she was draped in a sexy feminine little black dress.

She nodded silently.

They took seats in the large funeral parlor, set out with additional fabric folding chairs.

Matt always hated the scent of funeral floral arrangements. It smelled of formaldehyde and cheap perfume. Today only made worse by the abundance of painted scented women. Damien wasn't picky, Matt thought to himself. He wouldn't put his dick in any of these women. Well, maybe, one or two.

The priest spoke, although Damien wasn't a religious man. His captain gave a brief but touching eulogy. Damien's fiancé ,Faith, stepped up to the podium with tissues in hand. She began to speak.

Matt, Johnny, and Thomas were all startled by the depth of the masculine voice escaping her small five-foot frame.

Thomas leaned in, "Is that a guy? Jesus, it must be the steroids." He paused. Matt and Johnny smiled still facing forward.

Faith said a few endearing words, professing her love and dedication to him, her hopes and dreams for their future, gone. Damien's daughter and ex-wife stirred uneasily in the front row seats.

Then Faith made a few jokes about his obsession with technology and that in light of that she would like to share a power point presentation of what she'd like to call "All About Damien". Lights were dimmed, his cell phone was hooked up to a laptop, and the 'show' began. It was a slideshow of all the photos in his phone, a mix of copied text conversations from coworkers, friends, lovers, pictures of the boat, his daughter, family, friends, lovers, scantily clad or naked women, some of them on the boat, his daughters photo with a caption 'she's so fat', it continued and people stirred uneasily. Nobody was sure how to react.

"Do we stop it?" They were so titillated by the dark and secretive nature of it, hard to look away. Damien's father stood up but sat back down, even he was intrigued.

Faith stepped away from the podium and strode elegantly to the casket and slapped his fat face with all her might. Which was a lot. The firefighters charged and grabbed at her.

"You bastard! You fucking bastard!" She screamed as three of them struggled to drag her out. Nobody stopped the flow of pictures as women slowly stood and slipped out the back doors.

"Well this is the best wake I've ever been to." Thomas smiled. "Definitely steroids, though."

Now just Matt, Johnny, and Thomas.

Peter doesn't show. Jason remarks that it is out of character, Peter usually calls if he's not coming. He suggests they wait a few minutes before they begin. Everyone is nervous and quiet.

Matt says, "Should I break the ice here?" he laughs. No one else does. "Just kidding, too soon?"

Jason begins to coax them into discussing their feelings.

Johnny states, "I'm glad he's dead. He was trying to fuck my wife."

Matt nods in agreement.

Jason asks, "How did they know each other?"

Silence.

Matt breaking the silence, "Sorry man, he had no chance with her, Johnny."

Thomas directs an accusation at Matt, "Its you."

"Me what?"

Thomas suddenly frightened by this realization says, "I quit. This feelings lounge rant is bullshit." He can't say anymore because he is culpable of a crime he can't even recall. Matt and Johnny know that Thomas won't say anything, he has a reputation to protect. Thomas can't confront them. His blood pressure rises and he is sweating heavy with anxiety.

Jason coaxing him to stay, states, "It's a difficult time for all of us."

Thomas looks from Matt to Johnny and back again. They are wide-eyed and knowing. He is stifled. He is helpless. Thomas stands and flings his chair. He paces, "Fuck you Jay!" He leaves slamming the door.

"Bye." Matt giggles that Thomas used his 'Jay' as a sign of disrespect.

Johnny talks about his loving wife and he's sad about the pain he's caused her with that "game".

Jason confused "What game?"

Johnny "I'm a good man. ", sobbing, "I don't want to lose her, she deserves the best of me, which isn't much, but I want to…" Johnny rises, "I have to go." He shakes Matt's hand. "Thanks man."

"No problem. I'll see you later Johnny."

Jason calls out to Johnny in his motherly tone, "Where are you going Johnny?"

"Home." He walks out confidently. He hasn't felt this strong, this empowered in a long time. He likes it.

Jason is staring at Matt. "I guess this will be a private session for you Matt." He pulls Matt's file and wants to discuss his anger issues. In his sweet feminine nurturing voice Jason asks about Matt's relationship with his mother.

Matt asks, "Can I use that bat?"

"Yes." Jason encourages Matt's willingness to express his emotions physically.

Matt pummels Jason with the padded bat. Jason is screaming like a girl begging Matt to stop. He is lying on the floor whimpering, "Matt, stop, please stop." He's sobbing and says, "I'm sorry, Matt." repeatedly.

"Yes, Jason, that feels much better, Mom."

Jason is bruised and embarrassed. He watches Matt walk out.

SONG SEAHAVEN SOLAR ECLIPSE

Johnny feels as if he is alive again, but this life is somewhat surreal. It's as if suddenly every motion, every sound, every breath is in slow motion.

Johnny arrives home early. The kids are still up. He is welcomed with hugs and lifts them up spinning, and smiling. They laugh at his tickles and kisses. Annie watching from the hall in her pajamas is smiling. He gently puts the kids down and pats their butts to go up to bed.

His eyes sparkle and his chest broadened, he stood erect. She missed him. She recognizes this man, the one she fell in love with so many times over the years, the one she loves more than ever now. Annie welcomes him with a sensual embrace and warm wet kisses. His strong arms squeeze her closer. Tears fall on his chest from the soul of her eyes.

He kisses her forehead and sweet adoring words are exchanged between them. They sit comfortably on the beat up couch holding hands. She rests her head on his shoulder. Warmth fills him.

He blinks with the sudden realization that Thomas is right about Matt.

"I have to go." He jumps up urgently.

"What? Why?" Annie is baffled.

"Honey, I can't tell you now, but I will. It's important. I'm sorry." He grabs his jacket over his shoulder. "I love you. Remember that."

"Johnny, what's going on?" She's upset he's leaving but she knows him well enough to let him go.

"I'll be back. I love you." He kisses her forehead again.

"Okay. I love you. You know that."

"Yes." He smiles, "Yes, I do."

(Seahaven- Solar Eclipse continues)

Johnny arrives and finds the door open, lights on and Jason sobbing at his desk.

Jason is reading Matt's file for the first time. He recalls the argument that distracted him and sobs more deeply.

Johnny reads over Jason's shoulder, sees the file out. He pats Jason on the back lightly. He copied down Matt's address and headed over there.

He arrives at a beat up house with multiple apartments and asks an old black man chatting with friends around a fire pit on the front lawn.

"Where's Matt?"

"That fine white boy? You one of his military buddies?"

Johnny nods his head, "Yes sir."

"He's a fine young man who served our country." He salutes Johnny. Johnny doesn't know the appropriate response so he awkwardly salutes back.

"He ain't home, but you can go on in and wait for him."

The old run down house was neat but not very clean with a shared living room, kitchen, and bath by a few residents. They direct him to Matt's room while staring at the television. He finds Matt's room upstairs. Being a mechanic, he jimmies open the lock and turns on the light.

Johnny studies the surroundings of the plain gray modest room. Newspaper clippings of all freak deaths including Bill, Damien and the as yet unidentified Peter are thumb tacked to a wall. A small dresser held one desk lamp. One laptop is open. Dog tags lay under the lamp on a bible. A blue duffle bag and knapsacks filled with small work and codes neatly stacked at the foot of the crisply made navy blue twin bed. Clear plastic storage bins are stacked and labeled with large assortment of computer equipment.

Johnny sits on the only chair in the room and turns on the laptop. A picture of a folded American flag held between white gloves is the background screen saver. A pass code is required. Johnny closes it.

Johnny realizes a shadow is cast into the room from the dim hall lighting. Matt is in the doorway. Johnny slowly rises. Matt has a pistol pointed at him. Matt shuts the door with his foot, gun still on Johnny. He shouts, "Sit down." Johnny does as he is told and steps backwards and sits on the bed.

Johnny asks with a shaken voice, "What's going on man?"

"You know, what's going on, played the game." Matt grins.

Johnny appealing to Matt's humor, "I think you won."

"Not yet"

Johnny promises, "I wont tell anybody."

"Wrong answer." Matt states firmly. Matt calmly and clearly explains, "I want to go away. I want to get taken care of. That's all I want is for them to think I'm crazy."

Johnny remains still and straight faced, "I think your crazy, Matt."

"You mean that Johnny?" Matt smiles warmly.

"Yeah man. Your as crazy as they come Matt"

Matt asks gently, "Would you swear to that Johnny?"

"Sure, Matt, whatever you want."

Matt commands him, "Put your hand on the bible."

Johnny realizes he has his hands in the air and asks, "Which one?"

Matt instructs, "The left one, you can leave the right one up."

Johnny obeys.

"Now swear to it." Matt continued.

Johnny unsure, "To what?'

"Swear I'm crazy"

Johnny states clearly, "I swear you are the craziest ass bastard I've ever known Matt."

"Thank you Johnny!" Matt rushes to hug him weeping, the gun is by Johnny's head and they rock back and forth on the bed. Matt is crying heavily. Johnny's eyes are open wide, as he hugs him back nervously.

Johnny asks, "Are you going kill me, Matt?"

"Kill you Johnny?" Matt giggles and releases Johnny from the embrace. Matt leans forward with his elbows on his knees, fiddling with the gun in his hands. "Don't be ridiculous. I can't kill you Johnny. You're my witness."

Johnny leans forward as well, "Oh that's good."

"Oh Johnny, don't be silly. You're going to swear right. In court I mean, that I'm crazy, right Johnny? You're a good guy. A true friend."

"Yes Matt."

"Thank you man." Matt puts his hand out and they shake hands. Matt pats Johnny on the shoulder, "Good man."

Johnny sits a moment in an awkward silence. "Alright, ummm.... I'm going to go now. You take care of yourself, Matt. "

"Yeah, yeah, yeah. Of course." Matt waves his hand happily, "You go do what you've got to do. I'll be here."

"Okay." Johnny gently walks to open the door. He looks back at Matt.

Matt waves him to go, "Go.".

Johnny drives away frantically. He pulls over with hands shaking calling the police and giving address information then hangs up. He pauses a moment and says aloud to himself, "Holy shit! Holy Shit! What the fuck?" he laughs on the ride home.

CUT TO NEWSCLIP

Matthew Hall is found guilty by reason of insanity for the murders of...

Sitting on couch in the mental hospital patient lounge, Matt is watching "My Fair Lady".

A woman's voice addresses him, "This is my favorite movie."

Matt turns and faces her, "Yeah."

"It won the Oscar the day I was born." She adds proudly. She offers him a hand full of junior mints by holding it out to him.

"Thank you." He responds as she pours a few counting up to ten.

"Is that enough?" she tilts her head coyly.

He pops them all in his mouth at once, "Yes", he replies mumbling with the mouthful.

They giggle.

'All I want is a room somewhere, far away from the cold night air....' Plays on the television as they stare at the screen.

"Want to dance ma'am?", he stands and holds his hand out like a gentleman.

"I'd love to." She gives her hand and rises with a courtesy. They begin to sway.

Matt and Rebecca dance happily. The song plays on.

THE END